LUKE ELLIOTT
A Young Texas Pioneer

By John W. Hamlett

With Illustrations By
Stephen Adams

*To Lathan

Enjoy!

John W. Hamlett*

authorHOUSE®

AuthorHouse™
1663 Liberty Drive
Bloomington, IN 47403
www.authorhouse.com
Phone: 1-800-839-8640

© 2011 John W. Hamlett. All Rights Reserved

No part of this book may be reproduced, stored in a retrieval system, or transmitted by any means without the written permission of the author.

First published by AuthorHouse   04/26/2011

ISBN: 978-1-4567-5307-8 (e)
ISBN: 978-1-4567-5308-5 (hc)
ISBN: 978-1-4567-5309-2 (sc)

Library of Congress Control Number: 2011903869

Printed in the United States of America

Any people depicted in stock imagery provided by Thinkstock are models, and such images are being used for illustrative purposes only.
Certain stock imagery © Thinkstock.

This book is printed on acid-free paper.

Because of the dynamic nature of the Internet, any web addresses or links contained in this book may have changed since publication and may no longer be valid. The views expressed in this work are solely those of the author and do not necessarily reflect the views of the publisher, and the publisher hereby disclaims any responsibility for them.

Dedication

For my students……

    Past and present.

Acknowledgements

Without resources an author is limited to what he can remember from his own recollection, but the early Texas history and that of the Civil War were events that happened just a little before my time.

My thanks to the following for providing accurate time lines and bits of history that made this story come to life:

David M. Fox for technical assistance
Luke Hamlett for cover photograph
Lone Star, A History of Texas and the Texans, by T.R. Fehrenback
The Handbook of Texas Online
The History Place
Wikipedia, The Free Encyclopedia

My Advisors

A very special thanks to several of my former students:

      Emma
      Brianne
      Calvin
      Josh
      Emily
      Abby
      Zachary
      Kelsey
      Debbie
      Vickie
      Luke

Contents

1. The Rise — 1
2. The Christmas Gifts — 11
3. An Early Age — 17
4. The Circling — 27
5. The Shawnee Trail — 35
6. The Kentucky Rifle — 47
7. A Deadly Shot — 63
8. Angry Discussions — 69
9. War Clouds — 79
10. A Difference of Opinion — 84
11. The Recruitment — 90
12. Hood's Texas Brigade — 97
13. Marching Orders — 102
14. Another Year Passes — 110
15. A Careful Aim — 118
16. The Promotion — 121
17. The Quiet — 130
18. Homeward to Texas — 134
19. The Running E in Sight — 144
20. A New Breed of Cattle — 150

Chapter One

The Rise

The battle of San Jacinto lasted only a few minutes. Less than twenty to be exact, but in that brief time a new republic was born. One that was to influence the rest of the world forever with its stories of greatness unmatched in history.

William Elliott, a rancher from the Hill Country of Texas near the city of Waterloo, had come to Texas with his parents, his wife Susanna, and his brother Sullivan with his wife Sarah as one of the "The Big 300" families led by Stephen F. Austin. They had brought with them their farm manager, Micah Jones, a free black man, and his wife, Lucy. Micah had been with them for years while in Virginia and was now the ranch foreman. William's father had built his cattle ranch, the Running E, from a small land grant into a 12,000-acre spread, one of the largest in the area. However, when his father's ill health forced him move into Waterloo, William had taken over the running of the ranch and its growth continued.

Now, however, William was a couple hundred miles away from his beloved ranch kneeling in waist-high grass along with a thousand other men waiting for General Sam Houston to give the order to attack the battle seasoned Mexican army only a few hundred yards away.

It was April 1836 that William found himself face to face with destiny along with Micah who went with him when the call for volunteers was sent out to join Houston in the quest for Texas' independence from Mexico.

Last month, the Alamo in San Antonio had fallen to the overwhelming Mexican army led by General Antonio Lopez de Santa Anna and all of the defenders had been killed.

A sense of terror gripped the people of Texas who feared the destruction they knew that Santa Anna was about to unleash wherever he led his army. The salvation of Texas was to be a renegade giant of a man and former governor of Tennessee who had seen more political battles than military ones. An impressive man standing at six foot three, Sam Houston had been appointed general by the congress of the newly formed Republic of Texas and was on his way to Gonzales, Texas, to take charge of the militia there with the intent of moving on to San Antonio to help defend the Alamo which stood in the path of the invading Mexican army.

Just outside Gonzales, one of Houston's scouts met Susanna Dickinson and several of the women survivors of the Alamo on a dusty road and brought them to General Houston. Susanna informed him that the Alamo had fallen to Santa Anna's overwhelming forces and related the story of the fate of its commander, William Barrett Travis, and all of the Alamo defenders. She had been spared by Santa Anna with the purpose of her spreading the word to the rest of Texas of the Alamo's fall and warning the settlers that he would offer "no quarter" which meant he would slay anyone who stood in his way as he attempted to eliminate the rebellion that was beginning to swell in Texas.

The garrison at Mission La Bahia at Goliad fell shortly thereafter with the massacre of James Fannin and the entire group of defenders by General Jose Urrea and his soldiers of the Mexican army.

Houston, with his collection of about 400 men, then ordered a retreat from Gonzales with instructions to burn everything of any value to Santa Anna who would soon be very close behind them in a chase to the Louisiana border and the safety of the United States some two hundred miles away. Beginning his march northeastward, Houston had hoped to pick up more men on the way because he knew he could not face Santa Anna's much larger army with so few untrained and undisciplined Texian soldiers.

Word began to spread of Houston's retreat and of the atrocities that Santa Anna had brought to the Texas settlers. Panic grew among them rapidly. Gathering up what few belongings they could carry and burning the rest, the settlers began a hasty race to the border in what was later to be called "The Runaway Scrape."

Houston began his trek to the east being questioned constantly by his soldiers as to when he was going to stand and fight Santa Anna and the Mexican army so close behind. Houston knew they were not ready for battle and tempers began to flair on a daily basis because he refused to listen to their demands to fight. Virtually none of the men had ever had any military training and knew even less of actual combat or following orders. Houston and a few of his officers were the exceptions. He knew that he had to be firm and began constant training of the now almost 1400 men in the art of soldiering.

The retreat continued towards the Sabine River and Houston knew that the time to fight for Texas was near at hand. He had withstood almost a month in retreat, rainy March and April weather, and constant griping among the troops. Bad as it was, his men continued to follow his lead. Houston now directed his men to an area near Galveston Bay where the San Jacinto River and Buffalo Bayou met and settled in preparing, at last, for battle. He was ready and the troops were itching for battle. Santa Anna's army had pitched their camp not quite a half-mile away…..and rested. Smoke from their campfires began to drift through the trees.

William Elliott was ready also. He carried his Kentucky long rifle, but had never shot at anything other than animals necessary for food. Now he was prepared to fire it at men across the grassy plain whose intent and purpose was to do to him a similar fate.

"Check your rifle, Micah, "William whispered, "and be ready to move out." Checking his own rifle, William propped it upon his right knee as he wiped the sweat dripping down from his hatband and into his eyes. "Never knew April could be so hot and humid."

Squinting across the grassy plain towards the rise, William tried to see if there was any movement from the Mexicans who may have been up there. Nothing. Only the gentle rustling of the grass. Scouts earlier had said that the Mexican camp was very quiet and that they seemed to be resting behind their barricade of brush, rocks, and saddles from the corral. "Resting?" William thought. "Surely, when General Houston gives to order to charge we'll give them a rude awakening!"

The tenseness of the coming battle was beginning to make its effect all up and down the line of the Texian soldiers who kept their eyes trained on General Houston waiting for the signal to advance. Houston, sitting majestically on his horse, Saracen, spoke quietly to several of his officers giving them their final orders. "Find me a bugle player," he said to one of the officers, "who can rouse this bunch of Texians who are so ready to fight." A few moments later the officer reported back and gave the reply "there are no buglers, sir."

"Well," Houston lamented, "we'll just have to do without one."

Overhearing Houston, a young soldier approached Houston and said in a quiet voice that only Houston could hear "I can play my fife, sir."

"Soldier," Houston grinned, "you are about to make history for Texas. Just what the Sam-Hill can you play on that thing?"

Sheepishly, the soldier replied, "not much, sir, but I do know one song and I think I can make enough of a noise that most of the soldiers can hear me."

"Good for you son," Houston grinned. "Get ready for my signal."

General Houston squared his three cornered hat so that it wouldn't blow off in the wind that was now sweeping across the plain. Houston pulled his saber from its sheath and raised it high over his head in a defiant manner almost as if to tell Santa Anna he was coming for a showdown with this man who so arrogantly called himself "The Napoleon of the West."

"Son," he said to the fife player, "play me that tune."

The breeze was now pierced by the high pitch of a tiny flute-like instrument as he played *Come to the Bower*, a rather seedy limerick often sung in bars. This time, the music was to call the Texian army to arms and would soon take its place in history of Texas' fight for independence from Mexico once and for all.

Houston now had his back to the San Jacinto River preventing any retreat from Santa Anna's army. Sending a squad of soldiers earlier to the banks of the river he had ordered them to burn the bridges that could have let them escape to the other side. They were now trapped, but Houston knew that Santa Anna and his army were tired and needed their siesta in the afternoon. Santa Anna, in his smugness, felt the same about Houston and his men……but Houston outsmarted him.

Shortly after three o'clock on April 21, 1836, General Sam Houston gave the order to advance.

William Elliott carried his Kentucky rifle in his arms prepared to open fire when they reached the top of the rise that separated the Texian army from the Mexican encampment. "Come on, Micah, follow me," William said as the advancing line of soldiers made their quiet approach to the rise just a few hundred feet away from them. The rise was protecting them from being viewed, but William knew that as soon as they reached its crest the Mexican army would sound the alarm and the fighting would begin.

Barely twenty-five years old, William Elliott had worked diligently over the last five years to build his ranch among the cedars and mesquite trees that flourished in the Texas hill country. He was one of the youngest of those that Stephen F. Austin had chosen to settle in what was to be called Austin's Colony, a land grant from Mexico established to ensure that it would continue to have a stronghold in Texas with political and religious leanings toward Mexico. Austin had been named Empressario of the territory.

There were other settlers in the area, each with ranches that were beginning to grow with every round up. William had grown up on a small farm in Virginia that had toughened his muscles during his younger years and given him the knowledge of business and the responsibility of working with the land. When his father learned that Austin was establishing the Colony, he decided to sell his farm and move westward to Texas to begin a new life in a part of the country that was still very much undeveloped and wild.

An impressive young man of a couple inches over six feet, but still a greenhorn in the cattle business, William had set about the tasks of ranching along with his father. He knew how to take care of animals and plant crops, but had not had the full experience of being in the business of ranching. They learned rapidly, bought a small herd of twelve longhorn cattle, and began to watch them grow into a much larger number as the years passed.

As was the custom in the frontier, everyone helped everyone else get established, build their houses, barns, and corrals. In fact, a barn raising was just about the only entertainment for the folks for miles around. Each gathering provided the opportunity for the men to pitch in to help build and for the women to prepare mounds of fried chicken, apple pies, and cornbread to feed the hungry workers. Along about suppertime, everyone gathered at the tables or on blankets to finish up the long laborious day with a bountiful feast.

William's thoughts of his home, the fireplace with its welcoming warmth, the smell of Susanna's cooking wore heavily in his mind as each step in the grass brought him closer and closer to the dangers of battle which could erupt in the next few moments. He hoped that Santa Anna's army hadn't gone northward as far as his ranch in his pursuit of Houston's army, but he knew that Susanna was well prepared to move further northward should the hostilities get too close.

"So far they haven't seen us," he whispered to Micah trailing behind him by a couple of steps.

The high-pitched fife continued to play its funny tune as the men picked up the pace to the point that they were now in a dead run almost to the rise. Just as the hundreds of men reached the top the Mexican army spotted them and bedlam spread through the camp as the soldiers tried to gather up their rifles they had so neatly stacked in a military manner before they began to take their siestas. Many Mexicans panicked when in the confusion of the battle their rifles became entangled with others and fell in a heap to the ground when they tried to arm themselves.

The Texians were now in full charge and from somewhere on William's right a loud voice was heard to yell, "Remember the Alamo! Remember Goliad!" The call was heard repeated over and over again as the Texians continued their charge towards the makeshift barricade the Mexicans had erected earlier in the day. Bullets began to fly from the Mexican rifles that some of the soldiers had managed to load and fire. William could hear them whizzing past, but hitting nothing but the humid April air. From behind on the rise came the loud roar of a pair of cannons nicknamed "The Twin Sisters", a gift from the people of Cincinnati, Ohio, that the army had received just a few days earlier.

A direct hit on the barricade blew a wide hole that would allow the Texians to rush through when they covered the next hundred yards to it. Three more blasts followed and three more wide holes appeared before the onrushing Texians ensuring them of an entry into the Mexican camp that by now was in total chaos. The Mexicans had been drilled to fight in squads, fire, reload, and fire again. The Texians hadn't been subjected to this manner of battle and chose to make themselves as small a target as possible by advancing as individuals, not as a group. They had but one purpose and that was to defeat this larger group by total surprise and by any unorthodox method they could think of.

William and Micah were now in a position where their shots would most assuredly prove deadly. William aimed at one Mexican who appeared to be aiming at him. His trigger finger was more rapid that that of the Mexican and William dropped him in his tracks. Able to reload in less than a minute, he dropped to his knee, placed the powder in the rifle, rammed the ball down the barrel, and fired a deadly shot once again. Micah was doing the same thing and his aim was equally as deadly as that of William's.

By this time, the Texians had broken through the barricade and had entered the Mexican camp which was becoming a bloody scene of hastily dressed Mexicans caught unaware that the Texians would dare attack in such a manner. The Mexicans were in full retreat, dropping their weapons, and running for all their might towards the river and the burned out bridges. The Texians dropped them like flies. The call to "Remember the Alamo, Remember Goliad" could be heard throughout the disassembled campsite and still the onslaught continued. Many of the Mexicans had made it to the river, but were drowned when they tried to swim to safety or were picked off by the Texians firing at them from the shore.

William and Micah stood in what had been the Mexican stronghold just moments before with unbelieving eyes as they surveyed the carnage and dismay before them. An elite Mexican army had just been defeated by a not so elite Texian army madder than hornets and determined to avenge what had happened to their fellow Texians just last month.

"Are you okay?" William asked Micah who was standing with his mouth wide open.

"Not a scratch, but I have a bullet hole in my hat from one of those Mexicans who couldn't get much of an aim at me. I fired at him at almost point blank range. Saw him tumble backwards like a mule had kicked him in the chest!" Micah said in a boastful manner.

Managing a sigh of relief, William gathered up his wits and began searching the camp for any remaining Mexicans. Others were doing the same and herded those they could find into an open area of the Mexican camp where the cooking pots still bubbled with untouched food.

Hundreds of Mexicans lay dead or dying at the end of the battle, but a Mexican bullet had killed only two Texians. William said to Micah, "I saw General Houston's horse go down, but the general got up and jumped on another one nearby. That one fell also and I think the general got hit in the foot because he was limping when he tried to stand up."

The battle was over, but Santa Anna was nowhere to be found. Houston was furious that this man, so pompous in his previous defeats of the Texians, had managed to elude capture when the Texians poured over the campsite.

The next morning, William was detailed by one of the officers to search the banks of the river to see if there were any remaining Mexicans hiding there. Mounting a horse, he set out towards the San Jacinto River to chase out any who may be cowering near the river. Much to his surprise, William found a group of about fifteen Mexicans squatting in the reeds, muddied by the banks, and terrified that this huge Texian on a horse was about to have them join their slain comrades.

"Ariba! Ariba! Up! Up!" William ordered the Mexicans. They all rose timidly lining up one behind another and began marching back towards the campsite they had just recently tried unsuccessfully to defend.

The prisoners were directed toward the assembly area already filling rapidly with stragglers in various stages of dress and undress. William reported to one of the officers that he had found these troops at the river and that they had not put up any more resistance. They seemed to be relieved that they had been spared and not met death as so many others had.

As William was turning the prisoners into the assembly area the other prisoners began to look at the newly arriving group, stood up, and shouted "El Presidente, El Presidente!" William was stunned and noticed that one prisoner was walking by himself wearing a jacket bearing the rank of corporal on its sleeve.

"Could this be Santa Anna?" William asked the officer in a rather excited voice.

"Sure 'nuff looks like him," the officer said. "I'll take this guy to the command post to see just who he really is" he added.

"Sure 'nuff," William chuckled to himself. It really was Santa Anna that William had captured down by the river and hauled back as a disheveled enlisted soldier and not as the leader of the Mexican army. "Sure 'nuff."

The plain white flag with the blue star symbolizing Texas had been planted in the middle of the campsite while over by the bayou General Houston was propped up next to a tree with his ankle wrapped in bandages from the bullet that had disabled him during the battle. Standing before Houston was a rather small Mexican who just a day before had been the leader of what he thought was an invincible Mexican army, but which now lay in defeat at San Jacinto.

William and Micah watched from behind the officers gathering around Houston and witnessed the final episode in Texas' fight for independence from Mexico. They both thought of those who had died at the Alamo and at Goliad and wished that they could have lived to learn that Texas was now free from Mexican domination and that those other battles helped to make this battle victorious.

"I wonder if anyone will remember this battle," William said to Micah in a hushed voice.

"No doubt they will," Micah offered.

Chapter Two

The Christmas Gifts

Christmas Eve 1841 came with a soft snowfall uncommon for the Texas hill country even though the wintry weather there could make even the heartiest of rugged Texans scurry from one place to another seeking a warm fireplace and a hot cup of coffee.

A crisp white blanket spread over the hills covering the branches of the mesquite and cedar trees with layers of snow causing them to bend almost to the ground with their extra heavy load. The moon hanging in a clear black sky shined brightly on the snow giving the appearance of almost being daylight. A jackrabbit with its tall ears pointing skyward came out of its hole in a tree hollow to begin its search for a patch of grass possibly hidden beneath a fallen branch. A screech owl perching high up in the top of a barren oak tree kept his keen eye on a field mouse watching every move it made contemplating whether to swoop down from the lofty limb for a try at catching its evening meal. A coyote struggles across the open pasture towards its den with great difficulty as its legs sink deeply into the snow almost up to its shoulders.

The ranch house of the Running E with its roof covered with the mantle of snow was aglow with lights from the kerosene lamps shining out of the windows with a bright orange cast upon the white ground. A column of smoke rose from the stone chimney seeking its freedom in the night air and casting an aroma of sweet smelling burning oak with touches of cedar limbs added to it.

A surrey was parked at the front porch of the house with an old black horse chomping on a feedbag of oats and tethered to the hitching post next to the steps. It had brought Doctor Calley, the local physician in from town to the bedside of Susanna who was ready to deliver a new baby to be born on this special night of the year. Sullivan's wife, Sarah, was in the kitchen with pots of boiling water at the ready and stacks of linens and towels folded neatly on the table. William was excited about the new arrival, but also very much concerned for Susanna because the hardships of ranch life had caused her to lose two infants during childbirth before. Things had been a little easier on her this time on the ranch and hopes were high that this child would enter the world with a long life ahead of it. Doc Calley placed his black bag full of his surgical instruments and medicines on the dresser next to the bed and assured her that everything was going to be all right and that he expected no difficulties with this new arrival.

William paced the floor of the living room so many times that Sullivan, sitting next to the fireplace, said, "slow down my friend. You must have covered half the distance between here and Waterloo over the last hour and you still haven't gained anything but tired feet." "Besides that, you're makin' me nervous, all that mumblin' and stuff" Sullivan added.

"I know, I know, Sully," as William called him, "but I'm just talking to myself tryin' to give myself enough courage to face the next hour or so" William said softly.

"She's gonna be all right. She's strong and besides that she's a Texan" Sullivan spoke as cheerfully as he could manage trying to help his brother, but secretly praying for the well being of Susanna and William together.

Another hour passed as William poured himself a cup of coffee that Sarah had brewed for him just moments before. "When is this going to end?" William asked to no one in particular. After a long silence, which had spread throughout the room, the quietness of the winter night was broken with the cry of a newborn baby coming from the bedroom where Susanna was. Jumping up from his chair and spilling the hot coffee all over his pants, William was met at the door of the bedroom by Doc Calley grinning from ear to ear excited with the news that Susanna was ready to see him and introduce him to his new child. Racing to her side, William kneeled softly by Susanna and kissed her gently on her forehead.

"Meet your new son, William" Susanna beamed to her husband.

William, with a tear of happiness falling from his eye, looked upon the tiny face peering out from the blanket wrapped around it. "I've never seen anything so beautiful in my life" he whispered to Susanna.

"Here, hold him" she says and hands the bundle to William.

"May I? Really?" William asks nervously.

"Of course you may! He won't break, hold him" she says, "he's your son, too" Susanna offered with a twinkle in her eye.

"He's so tiny" William noticed, "but I'll bet he'll grow to be a big guy and surely he's goin' to shake things up around here in the future".

"We haven't chosen a name for him yet" William said with amusement. "We can't let him grow up with no name, can we?"

Susanna thought for a moment and said "I'd kind of like to name him after my father. That is, if that's all right with you."

William once again looked into the tiny eyes of his new son, chuckled, and spoke softly to him "welcome to the world, Luke Elliott, welcome to the world and a Merry Christmas. You're the best Christmas present ever".

The moon continued to beam down upon the covering of snow, which now began to swirl with new cold winds out of the north. Not really a blizzard, but the temperature was cutting enough to necessitate an extra sweater and muffler under a rancher's greatcoat.

The bunkhouse that had been made into a cabin for Micah and Lucy was also aglow with light from kerosene lanterns. An old buckboard wagon was parked in front of it with the horse tethered to a pole. The horse stood on one foot and then another shaking the frost from its coat trying to maintain a better degree of warmth than what was at hand.

The visiting midwife, Mrs. Early, had been summoned earlier in the evening when Micah sent one of the other ranch hands into Salem with the news that Lucy was in the first stages of childbirth. Wrapping herself in her overcoat, a hat with a turkey feather stuck in the brim, and a blanket from the stable, she hitched up her horse to her wagon and headed out to the Running E.

Once at the cabin, Mrs. Early, a tall, strong willed outdoors woman who had delivered dozens of local babies over the last several years, unwrapped the heavy blanket and coats from her shoulders and tossed them on a chair by the fireplace. "Maybe by the time I finish here those coats will be warm enough to get me back home" she chuckled.

Micah paced alone across the one room cabin floor time after time as he, too, wondered what was going on in the bedroom with the midwife and Lucy who was in the last stages of childbirth as well.

"Oh, my goodness, Lord" Micah spoke in a prayer. "Please help her through this time and keep Lucy well."

The coffee in the pot had turned cold, but Micah poured himself a cup anyway. It had the texture of the creosote that he and William had painted on the fence posts to protect them from termites and wood rot. Remembering the pots of hot water that Mrs. Early had asked him to start boiling, he dipped a spoon into one and added the hot water to his otherwise tar pitch flavored coffee. Adding a teaspoon of honey to the mixture, Micah thought to himself "I need some strength too."

Once again, the stillness of the cold Christmas night was broken by the cry of another newborn baby destined to help shape history. Mrs. Early came out of the bedroom and told Micah, who was standing nervously on one foot and then the other like the horse outside in the cold, "you may go in now. Lucy's waiting for you."

Micah beamed when he saw Lucy holding her new baby and he, too, leaned over and kissed Lucy on her forehead in a gentle and loving manner.

"We'll call him Joshua" Lucy said gleaming up at Micah.

"Joshua, Joshua. That was my grandfather's name and I am so thankful you chose that one for his name" Micah added.

Mrs. Early gathered up her now warm wraps, patted Micah on the back, and said to him "good fortune and Merry Christmas" as she mounted the steps to the wagon and motioned the horse to get moving towards her warm home again.

William, in his greatcoat, trotted quickly across the corral to the cabin to share with Micah and Lucy the news of his newborn son when he was met at the door by Micah beaming with pride with equally exciting news.

The two men embraced each other as only good friends can do each offering the other congratulations. They both were exceedingly proud to have become fathers for the first time.

Micah and William stood on the front porch of the cabin looking up at the moon still shining its daylight glow on the snow.

"Merry Christmas, Micah", William spoke.

"Merry Christmas, William", Micah added.

Chapter Three

An Early Age

In the almost twenty years since Texas had won its independence from Mexico at the Battle of San Jacinto, it had become a republic, a separate nation, but with strong ties to the United States. The small town of Waterloo had its name changed to honor the man who was later to be called The Father of Texas, Stephen F. Austin. Texas had its own ambassadors in different countries and the French had established theirs in Austin. Settlers from all over America began to arrive bringing with them their customs, traditions, and especially their foods all of which were blending in to create a new way of life. Now, the city of Austin was designated the capital of Texas having previously been located in Harrisburg and Washington-on-the-Brazos to a site just north of the Colorado River on the top of a hill overlooking Congress Avenue leading down to the river.

In 1845, Texas ceased being a separate republic and with much ceremony, the Texas flag was lowered in Austin for the last time. A nation that had fought for its independence through the battles of the Alamo, Goliad, and San Jacinto, had been recognized throughout the world as a new nation, had its own president was now to be read about in the history books forever as the twenty-eighth state to be added to the Union of the United States of America. The new flag of the stars and stripes which stood for another nation that had fought for its independence as well was now flying over the capitol in Austin.

The next several years were good years for the cattle business with herds getting larger with each roundup and prospective buyers in Kansas and Missouri anxious to get all the beef they could get their hands on. The Running E ranch was now encompassing over fifteen thousand acres of prime hill country with abundant water from the rivers and creeks for the cattle and green grass almost as far as the eye could see. The herd of longhorns now numbered several hundred and the price of beef was climbing. It took a lot of beef to feed the hungry masses back east and William Elliott was anxious to provide as much as he could.

The original one room cabin built by William's father so long ago had been replaced with a sprawling ranch house that would have made most of the folks back east stand in awe of its beauty. There were not the stately white pillars and tree lined approaches to the homes that were so typical of the southern plantations, but rather the Running E's home had a long front porch with rocking chairs and a view of the western sunset that would have made most people very envious of this new way of frontier living.

The living room was filled with rustic, but very comfortable furniture, most of which was made right there in central Texas by wood workers who had come with Stephen F. Austin when the area was settled. A massive fireplace stood in the middle offering comfort on cold winter nights. The kitchen had all of the newest modern appliances including a wood stove that Susanna and Lucy cooked mouth watering dinners and an actual water pump built right inside by the sink to provide fresh water on a continuing basis.

For lighting, the candlesticks were still kept for emergencies, but had been replaced with kerosene lamps in every room each of which gave an abundance of light even on the darkest of nights. There was a fireplace in the big bedroom because the one in the living room was too far away to provide warmth on cold nights. As a rule, since the house was build with sturdy, thick logs the temperature in it throughout the year was very comfortable regardless of the outside weather.

The prospect of indoor plumbing was being talked about, but was still something to be considered in the near future. The trip to the outdoor privy was just a short walk out to the back of the house and on warm summer nights the pathway was lighted by the abundance of stars above.

However, on snowy winter nights, the journey seemed a great distance and often times the "chamber pot" was hauled out from under the bed instead of bundling up with heavy coats to go outside. The washroom did hold a tin tub, which was filled with warm water when a bath was taken on more than just Saturday night. After a long day in the saddle herding the strays it felt pretty good to soak with water up to one's ears

Wildlife was still plentiful with deer and turkeys seen in almost every clump of trees resting in the shade while the summer sun beat down upon the land. It is always a good summer in the hill country with Saturday night gatherings on the river complete with food, music for dancing, and flirting with all the young ladies from the nearby ranches.

It had been good years for Luke and Joshua who were growing like weeds and approaching their sixteenth birthdays in a couple of months. Luke was head and shoulders above his schoolmates already with no sign of stopping at that level. The school house nearby in the small community of Salem welcomed the students each day with the ringing of the bell and the school marm, Miss Erin, patting everyone on the head as they arrived with books and slates in hand to get ready for the day's lessons. Miss Erin had to reach high to pat Luke who usually would stoop low, grinning at her as he did.

Luke had taken to school quite readily over the years and excelled in almost every subject. He particularly enjoyed math because it helped him in keeping track of the cattle stock, the costs of raising them, and just how much each cow would bring on the market when it came time to sell them in Kansas. He just didn't take much to history lessons though because he said he couldn't relate much to what people did in the past, but had rather concentrate on what was to happen in the future. He did, however, find a fascination with Sam Houston because of the stories that his father, William, told him about when he served with him at San Jacinto and wanted to meet him in person someday when ranch duties would allow him to journey into Austin with his dad.

Slavery was still practiced throughout the nation and Negroes were not afforded the opportunities that white people had when it came to education and definitely not the privilege of attending any sort of public school like where Luke spent many happy hours. The mere thought of giving a black person the ability to learn was unheard of and the practice of keeping them isolated was commonplace.

William Elliott did not believe in slavery and even though Micah and Lucy had been the children of slaves who had been the property of William's father, he did not consider them as such. Instead he considered them as a part of his ranch crew who were all expected to do their part on an equal basis to keep the ranch running as a business where all would profit from its success.

Susanna had been a schoolteacher in Virginia before their move west to Texas and she was determined to see that Joshua could at least learn to read and write. Over the years, she had managed to teach him the basic fundamentals of an education and when he could read a chapter from a book without missing a single word she felt that her own education was again being used to its fullest

Joshua would come by the kitchen door at the ranch house each evening so that he and Susanna could sit at the kitchen table studying as much as they could cram into what usually was a session of an hour or so. As a result of his sporadic education at night, Joshua showed a keen interest in reading the poetry books that Susanna had brought west with her. Joshua thrived on these books and would read them for hours by the fireplace long after his family had gone to sleep.

Summer time provided plenty of opportunities for the two boys to gather up their fishing poles and head to Canyon River with dreams of catching the huge catfish or trout teeming in the cool waters. In the fall, Luke and Joshua looked forward to hunting deer for venison to hang in the smokehouse rafters and an occasional wild turkey for Sunday dinners.

Leisure time came to an abrupt halt each time when round-up season arrived. Early on, the responsibilities the boys were given included milking the cows early in the morning, cleaning out the horse stalls in the barn, gathering the eggs from the hen house, and getting dressed for school all before breakfast time. The long workday began very early on the ranch and lasted until sundown. After dinner, studies were accomplished and off to bed where sleep came very easily for everyone.

In September roundup began with the gathering of the herd that had been given free range all spring into a pasture where they were kept prior to the long drive up the trails to Kansas to meet the railroads.

Luke and Joshua both had learned to ride before they were six and by now were capable of handling all of the horses in the corral. When they were younger, saddling them had been a problem because the saddle was so heavy and had to be swung up onto the horse's back without causing the horse to bolt. Luke and Joshua learned that if one of them climbed up on the horse's rear, the other could hand the saddle up after the blanket had been put in place. Shinnying down the rear of the horse, the one on top would then crawl under the horse while the other held the saddle in place to fasten the straps on the other side. It was a work of art and the boys prided themselves in being able to accomplish this monumental task now with so little effort.

Each saddling was done with perfection with the exception of one time when Joshua had not tightened the strap quite tight enough. While he was riding, the saddle began to slide off the side of the horse carrying him with it crashing to the ground. Luke, of course, thought this to be hilarious and doubled over with laughter while Joshua picked himself up, dusted his pants off, and retightened the strap so that it would stay in place.

Joshua got even shortly after that when he put a cocklebur under the saddle blanket of Luke's horse, which caused it to buck angrily when Luke put his foot in the stirrup and climbed into the saddle. Flying through the air, Luke landed with a thud right smack in the middle of a fresh cow patty. This time it was Joshua's time to roar with laughter.

Recently, when the boys were almost finished finding stray cattle and herding them into the pasture, they spotted a bushy tailed fox running for all its worth across the pasture. "Lookit that" Joshua shouted to Luke. "Let's chase him before he gets out of sight in those trees down there" pointing to a grove of mesquite.

"I'm already on 'im" shouted Luke as he dug his heels into his horse's flanks taking off at a gallop in pursuit of the rust-colored streak heading for safety.

"I'll wager that's the same fox that's been raiding the chicken house and killing all those chickens" Luke called to Joshua.

Slowing his horse to a stop, Luke jumped from his saddle as the fox darted under the bushes and headed for the nearest mesquite tree. It must have known exactly where it was heading because the fox disappeared into a hole in the base of the tree where the roots parted just enough to allow the furry creature to hide. Following close behind, Joshua was almost out of breath when he caught up to Luke. Luke was a faster runner than Joshua and often beat him in a race to the river, but sometimes he would let him win just to keep things even and the friendship in good standing.

"He's right there in that hole and I can just see his tail between those two roots there" Luke chattered.

"I think I can reach his tail if I get down real close to the ground without scaring it" Joshua whispered.

Getting down on all fours, Joshua reached towards the tail thinking "this fox is gonna really be mad when I start pulling. I've got to keep those sharp little teeth away from biting me really somethin' bad."

Grabbing for the fox's tail, Joshua gives it a yank and the fox pops out of the hole like it was greased down with some of the pig fat from the smoke house. "Lookit that, Luke, I got him with the first pull and he didn't even try to bite me once" Joshua exclaimed.

"Ooh-wee", Luke shouts, "Papa's gonna be glad we caught him so he won't raid the chicken house again."

Untying a gunnysack from his saddlebag, Luke opens it real wide so that Joshua can drop the fox into it. "Grab that piece of leather on the side of the sack when you drop that critter into it and tie it around the top to keep him in it 'til we can get back to the ranch" Luke says to Joshua.

With the fox squirming around in the bottom of the sack, Joshua ties it off and laughs about the fact the fox is doing its best to figure out where it is and where it's going. Fastening the sack to the ring on the saddle, Luke makes sure there is no way for the fox to get away out of the sack.

Luke and Joshua felt pretty smug about their achievement and knew how glad William was going to be when he found out that the chicken thief had been nabbed by two such experienced hunters when they both begin to feel things crawling up their legs under their jeans.

"What, the….." Luke yells, looking down at his boots and sees hundreds of tiny specks beginning to crawl up his legs.

"They're all over me, too" Joshua cries and frantically tries to brush those that were already covering his boots.

Both boys looked as if they were afflicted with the St. Vitas Dance as they jumped, snorted, and fanned their arms trying to brush the invading horde of ticks that by now were making their way up to their shins under their jeans.

"I don't like ticks" Joshua shouts, "and I can't see them very well against my black skin. But I know they're there and they're givin' me the creeps."

Luke, thinking the same thing, but not admitting that he loathed ticks because they always could find the most inappropriate places in which to bury themselves.

"Yank your clothes off quick before they spread all over your body" shouted Luke who by this time had managed to get his boots off and was trying to loosen his belt to pull his jeans down.

Frantically, the boys both quickly knocked off dozens of the tiny black objects intent on finding a warm spot to dig into the skin and lodge themselves firmly. Just about the only way to get them off was to pick them off one by one, but it could cause a terrible itch and a sore for days if a part of them was left in.

"When we get back to the ranch, Mama will cover us with sulfur powder and that will get the rest of them" Luke remarked to Joshua.

Luke and Joshua suddenly realized that the only articles of clothing that they both were wearing were their hats and that their clothes lay in a heap on the ground still crawling with the ticks that managed to hang on after the brushing.

"I'm not going to put those things back on with all those things crawling around on them still" Joshua lamented.

"Just hang them up on the branches of the bushes and we can come back later and pick them up" Luke suggested.

"Good idea" Joshua offered, "and let's not forget to bring another gunny sack to put 'em in too."

"But what are we going to wear back to the ranch?" Joshua asks.

"Your birthday suit" Luke answers laughingly.

"Aw, gee, Luke, what if somebody sees us?" Joshua mutters in an embarrassed tone.

"Don't worry. We can ride into the barn and put on our coveralls that I saw hanging there earlier this morning and that way nobody will notice us at all" Luke offers.

Putting a bare foot in the left stirrup, Luke climbs upon his horse as Joshua does the same on his.

"We're a fine looking pair, but at least we got our hats on" Joshua laughs.

"That's very important, Josh, a cowboy is never without his hat" Luke agrees.

"I still feel like things are crawling up my legs" shouted Joshua.

"They probably still are, but you'll just have to wait until Mama can get the sulfur powder on us. I'm not stopping for nuthin' until we get there, especially to pick ticks off you when I can feel them still crawling up my legs too."

The two boys make a hasty retreat towards the barn with their rears shining in the breeze unaware that their every move was being observed by another horse rider sitting under a nearby tree.

"Well, my goodness" Elizabeth Wyatt mutters to herself. "Those two boys have gotten themselves into a passel of trouble all because of that silly fox and now they're heading back to the barn with nothing on but a smile!"

Chapter Four
The Circling

The August sun rose almost directly overhead reminding Luke and Joshua that lunchtime was upon them and a few minutes rest from riding the north pasture all morning was at hand. The gurgling in their stomachs was also a reminder and they both headed for the shade of the old red oak tree over by Prairie Creek.

Dismounting from his horse, Luke untied the canvas bag hanging from his saddle ring with anticipation of the bread and blackberry jam that his mother had prepared for the two of them for their lunch. "This is gonna be real tasty" Luke, licking his lips, said to Joshua, "and there's a couple of pears in here too."

"I'll get us some water from the creek and fill up our canteens" Joshua added. Walking over to the creek, Joshua unslung the two canteens from his shoulder and dropped them to the bank. Kneeling down on all fours, he placed his face and most of his head into the cool water and sipped in a couple of swallows before raising up to catch his breath. He let the water drain from his head onto his shirt which helped to cool him off even more.

Placing the two canteens into the water, Joshua went about filling Luke's first when he noticed a school of minnows swimming lazily about a foot away from where he had the canteen. Carefully moving the canteen closer to the tiny fish, the water being sucked into the canteen drew one of the fish through the top and inside. He quickly placed the cork back into the canteen with a chuckle and began to fill his own being very careful not to get a minnow in his. With a hidden smirk on his face, Joshua walked back to where Luke was setting up for lunch.

"We need to water the horses before we eat and then we can tie them to the bushes under the tree" Luke offered.

Taking care of his animal was the first thing a good cowboy always did prior to taking care of his own needs because the horse was the cowboy's sole means of transportation while riding the miles of a large ranch.

Letting the horses graze near the creek, the boys stretched out on the grass under the oak tree and Luke opened the sack full of sweet smelling bread that Susanna had baked just that morning and the blackberry jam from the berries he helped pick from the bushes that grew along the creek.

"Shoulda seen my hands the other day after I finished picking these berries" Luke said with a grin. "They were as purple as this jam since there were so many to pick from and I think I ate two for every one I put in the bucket I was collecting them in. Mama laughed at me when she saw my face because it was smeared all over with that same juice."

"Wouldn't show on my black face or hands" Joshua laughed. "No sir. Couldn't even see those blasted ticks when they were crawling up my legs either."

Having finished their lunch and leaning back on the grass with the big branches of the oak tree shading them from the hot sun, Luke and Joshua rested for a short while before they headed back out looking for the rest of the cattle and making sure they were all right. Luke opened his canteen to take a long drink of water before refilling it and as he emptied the last swig his eyes grew the size of dinner plates realizing something had been in that last drop. Coughing up a storm and spitting over and over again, Luke tried to figure out just what it was that he had swallowed when Joshua began to roar with laughter at the look on Luke's face.

Joshua calmed down and admitted to Luke that it was only a minnow and surely he had eaten fish before.

Luke retorted "sure I have but they have always been cooked! Just you wait Joshua Jones, just you wait! I'll come up with something to get even, you watch!"

Taking his canteen to the creek to refill it, Luke looked up into the branches of the tree as the sunlight flickered through them. "Will you lookit that?" he said excitedly.

"At what?" Joshua inquired.

"Up there," Luke pointed, "on that branch about twenty feet up there. Lookit at hornet's nest and lookit all those hornets buzzing around it just a comin' and a goin' like they owned the place."

"I recon they do at that" Joshua mused as he, too, spotted the nest.

"Come on….let's knock it down and see what happens" said Luke as he grabbed a small smooth rock from the creek bed.

"I don't know" Joshua added cautiously. "Maybe we'd just better leave it alone because they are really gonna get mad at us if we disturb their house."

"Well, I'm gonna try to knock it down so be ready to run if I do" Luke warned as he let fly with the rock which whirled by the nest missing it by a foot. "Aw, I missed with that one. Here, let me get another one" Luke grunted as he picked up a rock just a little larger than the last.

Taking a careful aim at the nest, Luke hurled the rock with all his strength hitting the nest dead center causing it to explode with hundreds of swarming hornets looking for something to vent their anger upon.

In just a few moments, the hornets sensed the two cowboys looking up rather sheepishly at what had just come about and directed their attention towards them with a vengeance.

"Run!" Luke yelled.

"Where?" Joshua screamed as a hornet landed on the back of his neck. Smacking it with his hand as another three or four buzzed around his face Joshua started to follow Luke's suggestion and run.

"Ow! Ow! Ow!" Luke cried as three hornets stung him in three different places. "The creek…..run for it."

Both boys hightailed it towards the safety of the creek with the angry hornets close behind them with an "Ow" yelled a couple more times by each. Hitting the creek at a run, they both dived under the water and paused for a short while hoping the hornets would have left by now.

Still wearing their hats and clothes, two heads popped to the surface at eye level and surveyed the area around to see if there were any remaining hornets buzzing over them. Not daring to leave the safety of the creek for a while, the boys contemplated their next move and that was to walk gingerly to the bank keeping a sharp lookout for any other hornets that may be lurking about still feeling ready for revenge.

"Looks like they've all gone" Luke said to Joshua. "Shoulda left them alone like you said. And these stings hurt like the dickens, but I'm glad we got so few. That could have been a really stupid thing."

"We're soaked to the skin" Joshua observed "and we've got the rest of the day to ride before we can head back home to some dry clothes."

"Well, in this sun it won't take them long to dry and besides now we won't have to take a bath tonight because we've already been in the water" Luke chuckled.

Heaving themselves up on their horses, Luke and Joshua headed out towards the part of the pasture they hadn't checked on earlier. The warm sun beat down upon them again and their clothes began to steam up almost as if they were on fire.

"I still feel like I'm sitting in a puddle of water" Luke lamented. "Hope these pants dry out before long because my rear is getting a little chapped rubbing up against my saddle."

"Do you see those turkey buzzards circling up there just beyond that next clump of trees?" Joshua asked.

"Been watching them for a while and they seem intent on staying there for a bit. Let's check it out" Luke called to Joshua.

Urging their horses into a slow gallop the boys headed toward the area the buzzards were showing so much interest in. "Hope it's not another cow down"
Luke said worriedly. "Saw one yesterday that the coyotes had gotten and pretty much had a feast on. Coulda been a cougar, too."

"I don't see a cow anywhere so maybe it's something else" Joshua called from a few yards away.

Observing the buzzards still overhead, Luke continued to search the grassy pasture and spotted a brown clump just ahead of him. Dismounting, he cautiously approached the creature on the ground and calls to Joshua "it's only a dead deer over here. But it's really dead!" Holding his nose from the smell he heads back to his horse when he spots something rolled up in a ball next to him and not moving a muscle.

"It's a fawn and it's a newborn one at that" Luke tells Joshua who is now approaching on his horse. "Would you lookit that!"

"That must have been his mother lying dead over there and here it is left all by itself" Joshua observed.

"We can't just leave it here, the coyotes will have it in a moment if those buzzards don't get it first" said Luke as he bends down on one knee patting the infant fawn with his hand.

Starting to shiver from fright, the fawn lifts its head up and tries to stand, but its wobbly legs wouldn't let it remain upright but for a few moments. Gently placing one arm around its hindquarters and the other in front of its legs, Luke carefully picks the fawn up as it struggles to get free from his grasp. "I'm going to take it back to the ranch and feed it because it probably hasn't eaten at all since it's mom died probably a couple of days ago."

Joshua dismounted and held the fawn as Luke put his foot in the stirrup and swung his leg over the saddle. "Here, I'll carry it between me and the saddle horn and it should be okay until we can get it home" Luke says.
"But we've got to finish checking out the north pasture before we head back, don't we" Joshua asks.

"Yep. We can do that on the way home and still finish what our jobs for today are" Luke added.

The fawn rested quietly in front of Luke as he and Joshua finished their ride to the north pasture and headed back to the ranch house. All the while, Luke is mulling over and over in his mind just what was he going to do with this creature of the wild. He couldn't just turn it loose because it wouldn't last a day without its mother to look after it and besides he didn't have a pet at all to call his own. Maybe this could be it, he thinks.

Riding into the stable, Luke and Joshua taking the saddles off the horses, placed their mounts in their stalls and hung the saddles and bridles in the tack room. Meanwhile, the fawn had been gently placed on a bed of hay in a pen and hadn't stirred for the last several minutes while the horses were being rubbed down and fed.

"Lookit what I found, Mama" Luke showed his mother the bundle that he carried in his arms. "Found it in the north pasture alongside its dead mother that some coyote or cougar had gotten a day or so ago and I just couldn't leave it alone for sure it would have been eaten by that same cougar or coyote or those buzzards that were circling overhead where we found it and isn't it cute and can I put it in the barn with the rabbits so it won't be eaten?" Luke exclaimed all in one breath.

Susanna, looking at the brown eyes of the fawn remembered looking at the brown eyes of Luke when he was just born and thinking what a beautiful thing that God had given her. "I think your father wouldn't object to your having a pet and I certainly wouldn't either just as long as you take care of it" she said wiping an unseen tear from her own brown eyes.

"Oh, yes ma'am" Luke cried with glee, "I'll take good care of it. You know I will."

Cradling the fawn in his arms, Luke took it back to the barn to the pen where the rabbits lived over in the corner. Placing the fawn in the pen, Luke went about finding a bottle and filled it with several squirts of milk from the cow in the next stall. He dipped his little finger into the milk and held it up to the fawn's mouth as it hungrily lapped it with its tongue. Doing this successfully several times, Luke took a small rag and stuffed it into the neck of the bottle and tried to get the fawn to suck on the milk-laden rag for a change. "Now, you've got the idea" Luke thought to himself as he watched the fawn drink the bottle dry.

Rearranging a small pile of hay in a quiet corner of the pen, Luke picked up the fawn and placed it upon it with care. Noticing that the fawn is a doe, Luke thought to himself she must have a name.

"Jody. Your name will be Jody" as Luke patted the fawn on the head and scratched it behind her ear. "Sleep tight, Jody. I'll see you in the morning."

Chapter Five
The Shawnee Trail

When the summer of 1857 brought its warm afternoons to the hill country, Luke, in his sixteenth year, was already sprouting past six feet tall and from the looks of things would probably catch up to his father's height in another year or two. He had inherited the handsome looks of his father, the grace of his mother, and his curly blonde hair and brown eyes made him one of the most popular youths in the area.

Roundup time was always an exciting event at the Running E, but it involved hours of being in the saddle searching the far reaches of each pasture for cattle which were probably doing their best to hide in the shade of the many mesquite trees. Somehow, they sensed that they were about to be taken on a long, long walk northward to Kansas and Missouri.

After the cattle were herded into the retaining pens, branding time would start for those cattle not already having the Running E brand on their haunches. The ranch hands, now numbering eleven, prepared the fire pits near the corrals and placed the branding irons in them until they turned white hot and ready for the mark that would forever identify that this cow belonged to the Running E. Luke wasn't particularly fond of this part of ranching, but he managed to carry his weight with the other cowhands who were a little more experienced in getting the unmarked cattle separated from the herd, wrestled to the ground, feet tied together, and the mark applied to a loudly protesting cow. He and Joshua usually worked as a team and would alternate who would apply the hot iron to the hide.

"That stinks," Luke often commented as he held the branding iron on the hide for no more than a few seconds insuring a permanent mark. Joshua agreed that being in the same pen with a lot of smelly cows was better than this burning aroma ever could be.

When it was all done, Luke and Joshua would pat themselves on the back and admit that they had done a pretty good job. Many times the older cowhands agreed that the two of them were developing into mighty fine "cowpokes."

Already saddle seasoned from riding since they could just barely walk, Luke and Joshua had made two cattle drives north to Kansas with their fathers and the other ranch hands learning more and more with each experience that cattle raising was a very lucrative way to make a living, but an extremely hard one. Riding "trail" was the one place Luke and Joshua hated on the long drives because it was their job then to follow along at the rear of the herd having to breathe the huge clouds of dust churned up by the moving cattle while making sure that the stragglers were kept with the rest of the cattle. They would pull their bandanas up over their noses to keep from breathing too much dust, but their eyes suffered constantly from the stinging dirt causing tears and creating rivers of mud on their faces. On the cattle drives there were always the dangers of stampedes which the longhorns were prone to do, nasty, cold weather, rustlers along the way, and sickness while on the trail. On one drive, a thunderstorm caused the loss of almost two dozen prime steers when a sudden bolt of lightning startled them into running in a dead heat for almost four miles before the drovers could turn them and calm them down. That one lasted almost all night long and when sunup came, the riders were almost exhausted from the chase. William, knowing that to prod them into riding on that day would be unwise, chose to delay the drive for a day to give them some much needed rest.

Luke not only had his duties as a drover, but he liked to help the cook set up the evening meal. While on the trail, he became pretty adept at cooking by learning to prepare roasts in a Dutch oven, boil potatoes in a huge pot hanging over the cook fire without spilling them, the secrets of making delicious biscuits, and the ability to mask the constant taste of pinto beans into a tasty meal. His biggest success was making coffee that the drovers liked. The drovers told the cook to let Luke make it from now on since his tasted like coffee and not coal tar. The chuck wagon carried virtually all the food for a two month long drive and by the end of the trek the pickings were usually pretty slim with meals consisting mainly of biscuits and beans. Occasionally, William would tell "Cookie", as the hands all called him, to slaughter a steer to provide several days of choice beef for everyone. Once in a while, a drover would shoot a deer, which provided an additional different taste for the hungry men.

One afternoon when "Cookie" and Luke were preparing dinner at the chuckwagon, one of the younger cowboys decided he was going to show off a little in front of the more experienced trail riders by saddling up a horse known for its ill temper with certain riders. He was bent on proving he was as good as they were by letting this particular horse know that he was not going to put up with its bad temper and that he was the one to do it.

Throwing his lasso around the horse's neck, the cowboy tied it off to a tree limb to keep it steady. He should have paid attention to the fact that its ears were laid back flat, a sign that it was going to be very mad at whatever the situation. Ignoring this, the blanket was placed on the horse's back and then the saddle, which caused the horse to become jittery while the strap was placed under it and fastened to the saddle on the opposite side. The bridle came next and getting it into the horse's mouth was another difficulty that the cowboy had to contend with in his attempt to prove a point to the other cowboys.

By this time, some of the other cowboys had noticed the attempt to saddle the horse and began to gather around to see just what was going to happen when this young whipper-snapper made his attempt to mount up. Some of them knew very well that riding this horse was not to be treated lightly because several had been introduced to the hard ground when the horse had bucked them off in a rather ungentlemanly manner.

Putting his left foot into the stirrup, the young cowboy swung up and over into the saddle and pulled back on the reins after releasing the lasso from the horse's neck. Kicking his spurred boots into the flanks of the horse, it began to buck wildly attempting to throw this unwelcome rider into the dirt just like it had done to some of the others. Hanging on for dear life, the rider was successful in staying in the saddle for several strong bucks from the horse, but not before it had entered the cooking area where the evening meal was being prepared over the open fire. The clatter of pots and pans being kicked far and wide by the horse's legs, the spilling of the huge pot of beans, the coffee pot, the biscuits cooking in the Dutch oven, the cook fire scattered here and there, and the rage of "Cookie" as he came charging after the rider with a huge butcher knife in one hand and a meat cleaver in the other sent the observers into fits of laughter when the young cowboy was hurled several feet into the air as the horse made a fast twisting buck successfully dislodging him and throwing him to the ground with a thud.

"Cookie" was about to lay into the young cowboy trying to pick himself up and dust himself off when Luke stepped in and told him to get up and tend to the horse which had wandered off towards the other horses in the corral and not to make such a fool of himself again.

The cowboys had slim pickings for dinner that night.

The Shawnee Trail, which had been used long ago by the Indians as a hunting trail, was now followed by the ranchers from all over central Texas. The cattle were driven up through Austin and continued north towards Dallas and the Red River. Crossing over into Indian Territory, the herds were driven still further northward towards the railroads in Missouri and Kansas where they were penned in the staging areas for several days while being fattened up for market.

The drives usually went without too many incidents, but the longhorns carried with them the ticks that were so prevalent in Texas. The longhorns were immune to these ticks, but the northern cattle from the ranches of Missouri and Kansas were not. As a result, many of the northern ranchers' cattle died from a sickness later known as "Texas Fever." The Missouri and Kansas ranchers and farmers were violently opposed to any more Texas cattle coming through their areas and began forming armed vigilante groups causing many drives to be turned around. The Texas ranchers then had to find alternate routes that carried them more westward far out of their way adding days to the already long drives.

In Kansas City, William and Luke sat atop the corral fence counting each longhorn as it passed under them through the chute, which led them up the ramp and onto the waiting railroad cattle cars. "Three hundred and six, three hundred and seven, three hundred and eight" counted Luke who was listening to his father count the same number just to make sure not a one was missed. "We're gonna be here all day counting….three hundred nine…. at this rate, but as long as they keep coming I'll keep counting…. three hundred ten."

As the last longhorn found its way into the chute, both William and Luke shouted out loud "one thousand five hundred twenty two" patting each other on their backs. "At twenty dollars per head that's over thirty thousand dollars" William added proudly. "It's been a good year" Luke said beaming.

"Now, let's head for home" William added climbing down from his perch atop the chute. "But first, lets let make sure the drovers are taken care of at the hotel and then let's you and me have us a hot bath and a big meal at the hotel café. Find Micah and Joshua and have them join us when they can."

"You won't have to tell me twice for that" Luke chuckled as the two of them headed across the street for a few hours of relaxation before the long ride home.

Upon returning to the Running E, the ranch hands were given their pay and allowed to head into town for several days. Most of them would return to the ranch after they had spent all their money on some pretty fast living in Austin or down in San Antonio and were anxious to get back to raising the next herd.

William Elliott had just finished placing several pieces of paper into an envelope when Luke strolled by the desk where William was working.

"I have some papers here that need to be delivered to the new ranch family across the north pasture and I'd like you to saddle up and take them over to Mr. Wyatt for me, if you will," William said.

"Who are they?" Luke asked quizzingly.

"New folks who have just purchased the ranch that used to belong to old Mr. Addison" William answered.

"When did they take over the ranch?" Luke asked again.

"The sale came about while we were on the drive a while back and from what I hear they are a real nice family. They've been there for a couple of months and are getting a good start on another herd of longhorns. They're from Mississippi, I believe" William explained.

"Just tell Mr. Wyatt that Uncle Sullivan had the deed written up and posted in Austin at the County Court House just like he requested" William added.

"Uncle Sully has been doing all right in Austin now that he has his legal practice going strong. Must have a lot of paper work for all the ranchers around here, right?" Luke commented.

"He's doing well and he asked about you yesterday when I saw him in his office. Now head on over there and take these to him, please" William requested.

"I'm on my way, but it's gonna take me until this afternoon to make the round trip up there and back, you know. It's close to four miles up to that place. Think you can handle things here while I'm gone?" Luke spoke in a teasing tone.

"Get gone before I take the broom handle after you, you young whipper-snapper" William said as he reached in the corner for the broom.

Good humor prevailed at the Running E and Luke loved to tease with his Papa and Mama whenever the occasion presented itself. Of course, today was no exception and Luke was glad to go take care of whatever his father needed to be done.

"Here", Susanna called to Luke. "I've packed some jerky and apples for you to take with you on your way."

"Thanks, Mama," Luke whispered to Susanna and kissed her on the cheek as he left. "I'll probably stop by Prairie Creek to enjoy this later today."

"Just leave the hornets alone" Susanna joked as Luke headed out the back door and strolled towards the barn to saddle up.

Placing a saddle on his horse no longer required the help of Joshua since he could now swing it up on the horse's back almost with one arm. Luke was now riding a beautiful palomino mare he called "Golden". He had purchased it from a rancher in Kansas City just prior to his departure from there this last trip and was extremely proud of her looks and gentle temperament. They had gotten to know one another very well on the long ride back home.

"Where ya goin'?" Joshua called from the next stall where he was rubbing down his horse and filling its oat bin. He was still riding the appaloosa named "Apple" because he thought the name fit the description perfectly. Micah had traded some corn and beef to an Indian family in Oklahoma a couple of drives earlier. Both the Indian and Micah thought they had out traded one another, but in the long run the trade was equal since the Indian's family was in need of food and Micah wanted to bring a new horse home to Joshua as an early birthday present.

"I'm on a secret mission with important papers for the general at his headquarters" Luke responded jokingly. "No, I'm delivering a deed of sale to the new ranchers that took over Mr. Addison's ranch when he moved back to Arkansas. I'll be back sometime late this afternoon. By the way, would you feed Jody for me please?"

"Sure, I'll be glad to. Well, I'm just gonna go fishing at the river for a while. See you when you get home and maybe I'll share some fish with you if I'm lucky" Joshua shouted as Luke rode out of the barn and headed north.

Having ridden for about an hour, Luke approached the large grove of oak trees, which marked the location of one of his favorite places on the whole, ranch, and the spring fed pool of crystal clear water. Here, the water gushed up from a very deep hole in the limestone rock and spilled into Prairie Creek that flowed southward for miles. The water was very cold, but on a hot summer day was always welcome as a refreshing relief from the heat.

Luke checked the branches of the tree for a hornet's nest remembering a time gone by, but not seeing any he tied off Golden's reins near the creek so that it could get a good long drink. Luke sat down on a flat rock near the creek and removed his boots and socks from some rather smelly feet. He then rolled up his jeans to his knees and dangled them in the cold water, which at first was almost too cold to withstand, but worthwhile for the moment. Tossing a rock into the deep pool, Luke watched it disappear as it went down, down, down for goodness knows how many feet. "I haven't been swimming here in almost a year" Luke thought to himself. "It's time for me to kick off these clothes and just hop right on in."

Stripping down to his altogether, Luke took a deep breath and jumped feet first into the inviting water below. "Je-ho-se-phat that's cold!" Luke yelped as he gasped for breath upon reaching the surface. The sudden coldness had practically taken his breath away. Swimming and splashing furiously for several moments, Luke's body finally became accustomed to the coldness and allowed him several minutes of pure relaxation as he floated looking up at the clear blue sky above him.

Later, uncoiling his lasso from his saddle, Luke tossed it over a low hanging branch of one of the oak trees near the water's edge and fastened the other end of it around the tree itself so that he would have a rope to swing out over the water. Holding on to the other end, Luke could swing far enough out to drop right in the middle of the creek each time with a yell as the cold water engulfed him.

Drying himself off by sitting once again on the flat, warm rock, Luke redressed, coiled his lasso, and opened the lunch bag that Susanna had packed for him revealing not only the jerky, but a couple of fried chicken legs left over from dinner last night. "Ummmm" Luke spoke out loud. "She knows I love fried chicken."

Having spent a few moments after lunch just sitting and enjoying the beauty of his surroundings, Luke muttered to himself "it's time I get moving on."

Tying off the lunch bag to his saddle ring, Luke hefted himself up upon Golden and continued his journey to the north towards the Addison ranch, the Lazy H. Mr. Addison had tried to make a go of ranching ever since he came here several years ago from Arkansas, but just had not had the desire to work so hard just to make ends meet. He put his ranch up for sale and headed back to Arkansas and the farm he had left behind. He had been a nice neighbor. Luke would visit with him occasionally when riding the north pasture and often would find him sitting astride his horse overlooking his ranch from a small hill nearby. He had told Luke way back then that ranching just wasn't for him and that he probably would pull up stakes and go back to what was most familiar to him.

Crossing over the northern boundary of the Running E, Luke made his way to a small road, which would lead him up to the ranch house. Turning the next bend, Luke was able to see the house clearly and headed Golden to the hitching post at the front entrance.

"Hello, the house" Luke called out before he dismounted. "Hello, yourself" came a voice from inside as the new owner, Mr. Stephen Wyatt, approached the door.

"Good afternoon, sir" Luke said. "I'm Luke Elliott from the Running E and I have some papers my father asked me to deliver to you today about the sale of the ranch."

"Step down off that horse, Luke, and welcome to the Circle Bar W", Mr. Wyatt came offering his hand to Luke. "Thank you for coming and you must be tired from your long ride from your place. How do you like the new name for the ranch?"

"I'm fine, sir, and it's a great name" Luke answered.

"Well, come on in and rest a spell anyway. Mrs. Wyatt has just made some tea and I think I smelled gingerbread cooking in the kitchen. Like some?"

Gingerbread was his favorite and who was he to turn down such a fine offer from a new friend. "Thank you sir, don't mind if I do."

"Here, have a seat while I go over these papers" Mr. Wyatt said motioning Luke to a big leather chair by the desk. "Jane, we have a guest" Mr. Wyatt called to his wife in the kitchen.

"Well, my goodness. You're the first visitor we've had in a couple of weeks" Mrs. Wyatt commented as she entered the room.

"This here is Luke Elliott. His father owns the Running E and had his brother Sullivan do up these deed papers for us giving us title to the ranch."

"How nice to meet you, Luke" Mrs. Wyatt said in a gracious manner that only someone from the deep south could do.

"It's nice to meet you, too, ma'am," Luke said jumping to his feet, "and welcome to Texas. I understand y'all came from Mississippi a while back."

"Yes, we had a farm just outside of Vicksburg, but when the opportunity came for us to come here we just had to try our luck at ranching for a change. Have a seat young man and I'll get that tea and gingerbread for you two" Mrs. Wyatt said as she disappeared into the kitchen.

"We had that farm for a while" Mr. Wyatt commented, "but my father had been a rancher in Jackson and I grew up there. I really missed riding the range when we became farmers and I really didn't like depending on the weather to make the crops grow."

"My father's family were farmers in Virginia and they didn't like it much either. That's why they came to Texas to begin all over again just like y'all are doing. Hope you can make a better go of this place than Mr. Addison could because it just didn't work out for him" Luke offered.

Studying his papers very carefully, Mr. Wyatt smiled a big smile when he finished reading all of them. "Well, that's that!" he joyfully said. "We are now the owners of the Circle Bar W, all done up and legal."

Mrs. Wyatt brought in a tea pot and a plateful of steaming gingerbread just out of the oven and set it down on the table before Luke. "Here, let me pour you a cup, Luke, and help yourself to the gingerbread" Mrs. Wyatt offered.

Taking a bite from one of the squares of gingerbread, Luke savored the sweet tasting goodness. Taking a sip of tea from his cup, he winced at the hotness of it and blew on the contents a little just to cool it off.

"Am I invited to this party, too?" came a soft southern voice from behind Luke making him turn around startled that someone else was here.

And there she stood. The most beautiful girl that Luke had ever seen in all of his sixteen years. Luke, rising from his chair, was awestruck to the point where he couldn't utter a sound.

She was wearing a light blue dress with flowers embroidered on the sleeves and her black hair hung midway down her back and tied with a blue ribbon. Her deep blue eyes instantly reminded Luke of the blueness of the springs he had just been swimming in as he stared straight into them. He couldn't think of a thing to say and just stood there with his mouth half wide open.

"Luke," Mr. Wyatt said, "please meet my daughter Elizabeth."

In only a manner that someone from Mississippi could speak, Elizabeth stepped forward and stood looking up at Luke's curly hair and brown eyes saying "Hi, cowboy. Caught any foxes lately?"

Chapter Six
The Kentucky Rifle

    Elizabeth Wyatt walked Luke out to his horse after he had finished his tea and gingerbread and bid the Wyatts goodbye with a promise that he wouldn't be a stranger to the Circle Bar W ranch. After the surprise meeting of their daughter and the immediate pulsating of his heart, a team of wild horses couldn't keep him away from a return visit. And soon!

    Luke was still having a hard time coming up with the right words to say to Elizabeth and kept coming up with silly comments like "it's a nice day" or "the cedars really smell good this time of the year". He kept looking down at those blue eyes, the depth of which seemed endless, and at her black hair, which occasionally blew over her shoulder in the gentle breeze.

    "I'd like to call on you again sometime……if that's all right with you, Elizabeth" Luke managed to say without mumbling like he had been smitten. Which he had!

    "Please come back real soon, Luke, I'd like to get to know you better and maybe we could have a picnic out by the creek down yonder" she said pointing out towards their pasture. "I feel as if I already know you having seen you before chasing that poor little defenseless fox and then doing some kind of victory dance afterwards."

    Luke blushed the color of an Indian Paintbrush when he realized again she had seen Joshua and him trying to get the ticks off of their legs and riding home literally barebacked! "I....um....we....um....had ticks crawling all over us....and....um....had to get them off."

Elizabeth laughed and said "silly. I fell off my horse into a red ant bed once and got covered with those feisty little critters. Talk about dancing around in a frenzy!"

Laughing and feeling a little more at ease, Luke mentioned to Elizabeth that next Saturday was to be the county fair in Salem and asked if she ever been to one before. "Not here, of course, but in Mississippi we had fairs each year that I loved to attend....especially getting to sample all that good food that goes along with it" Elizabeth answered. "Are you going?" she asked.

"Yes, by all means. My mother is entering her plum jam in one of the contests and I'm sure she'll win a blue ribbon. You know plums grow wild around here....and blackberries, too" Luke added. "I'm entering the turkey shoot with the Kentucky rifle that my father carried when he was fighting at San Jacinto with Sam Houston. Will you be there?"

"My parents had mentioned that they would like to come because it would give them the opportunity to meet the other ranchers around here. We've only met a couple in Salem, but you're one of the first to come by since we settled in. And I think my mother will be entering her apple pie in that contest, too" Elizabeth responded.

Luke, putting his left hand on the saddle horn prepared to lift himself up onto the horse when Elizabeth placed her hand gently on his hand and said "will I see you there, too?"

"I wouldn't miss it for the world" Luke responded looking again into Elizabeth's deep blue eyes. "I can hardly wait and I will see you there, Elizabeth" as he swung himself up on his horse.

"How old are you" Luke asked trying to delay his departure in any way possible and fearing that she was going to say she was already twenty or something.

"I was sixteen in May. How about you?" Elizabeth asked.

"The same…..only my birthday was last Christmas Eve" Luke said.

"What a really nice time to have a birthday" Elizabeth commented.

"I'll see you Saturday, Elizabeth" Luke spoke as he urged his horse on out the gate and towards home.

"Looking forward to it" Elizabeth shouted as Luke waved his hat above his head in a goodbye gesture.

Luke could hardly wait to get home to share the news about meeting Elizabeth at the Wyatt's ranch. "Joshua will be anxious to hear all about her, too" Luke thought to himself.

A couple of miles from the Running E Luke began to come out of his daydreaming about the good fortune of the day and meeting Elizabeth. He stood up in the stirrups and at the top of his lungs sang out at the top of his voice "yeeeeehaaaaa!, yeeeeehaaaaa!, Luke Elliott's in love and I want the whole world to know about it!"

"Well, now!" came the voice of his father who had ridden up behind Luke while his head was in the clouds. "That's interesting news and I'd like to know what's gotten into you all of a sudden. I send you off with some legal papers and you come back like you've been into the cider keg" chuckled William.

Once again, Luke turned the color of a wild strawberry growing down by the creek when he realized his father had witnessed his announcement to everyone within earshot of Elizabeth.

"Oh, hello Papa. I didn't hear you ride up behind me. Been there very long?" Luke asked.

"Long enough to have my ears ring from all the yelling. I was up in the north pasture and saw you coming down the way and assumed that your visit to the Wyatt's was satisfactory and that you had delivered the papers to him" William answered. "Now tell me, just what was all that shouting about?" he asked quizzingly.

"Papa, I delivered the papers to Mr. Wyatt, who's really a very nice man and his wife is also, a woman I mean, that is" Luke offered clumsily, "and she served me some tea and hot gingerbread while Mr. Wyatt studied the papers and when I was almost ready to leave the most amazing thing happened."

"Well…. what?" William pressed for an answer.

"They have a daughter who's just my age and she came up behind me when I didn't even know someone was there and startled the wits out of me because…." Luke explained.

"Whoa, whoa" William said, "just slow down and take it from the beginning once again and tell me all about it your tea party with the Wyatts."

"Well, Papa, her name is Elizabeth and she knows how to ride and is going to be at the county fair this weekend when we are and…." Luke adds after a long pause "she's gorgeous….. and has invited me to come back for a picnic out on the creek soon." Luke said with a sigh.

"Well, that's really nice, Luke, and I'm delighted to hear that. I have only talked to Mr. Wyatt one day in Salem when he was trying to get the sale of the ranch taken care of. That's when I told him of Uncle Sully's law business… and you know the rest. We'll look for them at the fair this weekend" William offered.

The two rode into the barn and stepped down from their horses. "I'll rub them down and feed them, Papa, and will be up to the house in just a little while," Luke said.

"Thanks, Luke. Check out the left front shoe on my horse for me please. It may be a little loose because he was favoring it a bit a while back when I was out in the north pasture" William said as he left the barn.

"Well, welcome back" Joshua greeted as Luke was pulling his saddle off his horse. "Caught some fish this afternoon. One of them put up a big fight and I almost lost him, but I outsmarted him and before he knew it I had him on the riverbank" Joshua boasted proudly. "What'd you do today?"

"Oh, nothin' much" Luke commented as he inspected the horse's shoe, tapping the loose nail with the shoe hammer. Just delivered some papers to Mr. Wyatt, had some hot gingerbread, and met the most beautiful girl I've ever seen in my whole long life and all the way home I couldn't think of anything but her" Luke spoke with a glassy eyed stare when he remembered Elizabeth touching his hand before he left.

"You what?" Joshua asked with a half smile on his face. "You've gone and done what?"

"I think I'm in love" Luke continued with his faraway stare, "and I'm going to see her again this weekend at the fair."

"Well, by cracky. You've got a sweetheart and that's the best news I've ever heard. What's her name?" Joshua inquired.

"Elizabeth….Elizabeth….Elizabeth" Luke repeated in almost a singsong voice. "And all I could think of on the way home was Elizabeth."

Finishing up tending to the horses, Luke says to Joshua, "I'll tell you more tomorrow…..wanta go fishing in the morning again?"

"You know I do" grinned Joshua glad to have his friend back home with such good news.

****

Saturday morning arrived none to soon because Luke was anxious to load up the wagon and head to the county fair, which was just starting today. Helping William hitch up the horse, Luke patted it on the neck and fed it the apple he had picked up off the ground earlier. "Good boy" Luke said affectionately.

"So you're going to try your luck in the turkey shoot today" William asked.

"Yes, sir, I think I can take that prized blue ribbon this time without any problem like I had last year when the damp weather fouled up my powder causing me to flinch at the last moment" Luke lamented. "This time I'm ready!"

After placing the last of the apple pies for the competition safely in the back of the wagon, Susanna placed her foot on the wagon step and climbed aboard to her seat with Luke's help commenting "I'm ready, too!"

It was about an hour's journey from the Running E to the small community of Salem where the fair was to be. The sun was already breaking over the trees that lined the road into town and the early start was refreshing with the morning breezes just beginning to rustle the leaves.

"Gonna be a great day today" Luke said with a double meaning. "I hope to get off a few practice rounds before the actual shooting competition starts." Luke mumbled to himself under his breath "and I'll get to see Elizabeth again."

Riding into Salem, the streets were busy with folks going about their Saturday business and William pulled up in front of the General Store where he needed to pick up some supplies for the ranch.

"Need some nails and a new hammer" William said as he tied off the reins to the hitching post. "Broke my other hammer the other day when I was repairing the roof on the barn" he added.

Susanna and Luke both climbed down from the wagon and decided to step into the store as well just to look around. She went first to the dry goods area to check on some cotton material she needed to make herself another dress for everyday wear. Her other dress was getting a little tattered and Susanna was embarrassed to wear it anywhere but to do her household chores.

Luke always liked to revert to his childhood and headed straight to the hard candy display where huge containers of peppermint and licorice jaw breakers were in abundance. Being sold for two for a penny, Luke forked over a nickel and carefully chose ten pieces, five of peppermint and five of licorice for enjoyment after dinner later and back home while out riding the pastures.

Luke noticed a new display of firearms in the corner counter and his eyes fell upon a new Cold Navy Revolver that glistened in the morning sunlight shining through the window. His mouth dropped open a little when he admired the beautiful pistol and its leather holster just under the glass of the counter.

"Would you like to take a closer look at that?" spoke a voice from behind the counter. Luke hadn't even been aware anyone was there when he approached the gun display. It was Mr. Stuard, the owner of the store, who had been a family friend for many years and provided many of the necessary supplies to run the ranch. He was a tall, lanky gentleman with a very personable smile, always with a twinkle in his eye and a funny story to tell. He had two young daughters who helped in the store on Saturdays when they weren't in the same school that Luke went to during the week.

"Yes, sir, I would very much like to see it" Luke chattered anxiously. "I have never seen one like this before and I think it is probably the most beautiful handgun I have ever seen. I've fired muzzle loaded pistols before, but never one like this."

"This is one of Mr. Colt's newest inventions and has only been on the market for a few months. It came in yesterday in the shipment from Austin and from what I hear it is one of the best he has produced so far. Here, let me show you how it works" Mr. Stuard said as he bent low to retrieve it from the display case.

"This is a cap and ball revolver that uses the same principle as the muzzle loader, but the ball and powder are contained in the cylinder that will spin around to the next shot each time it is fired. It will hold six shots and can be fired as rapidly as you can pull the trigger. The hammer strikes this small cap here at the back of the cylinder and ignites the powder in the chamber. Isn't that a beauty?" Mr. Stuard said proudly.

"My! My!" Luke whistled as he held the gun in his hand. "It's so light compared to others and I bet it would be quite the gun to have on your side when confronted with rustlers on the drives up north", Luke added. "What does something like this cost, Mr. Stuard?" Luke asked.

"This one is ten dollars. A little expensive, but well worth the cost when protection is so important," Mr. Stuard offered. "One of the judges for the turkey shoot bought one yesterday to be used as the grand prize today for the one who can outshoot everybody else."

Luke's eyes glazed over in amazement. "You mean one just like this will be given away today at the turkey shoot here at the fair?"

"Yessir. And it will be a lucky fella who does win it" Mr. Stuard boasted.

"Well, I'll be" Luke uttered, as his mind was already thinking of the contest he was already planning to enter.

Susanna had already purchased some yardage for her new dress when an unusual glass jar caught her eye. Picking up an example of the newest of canning containers, she noticed the strange new lid to it that actually would screw onto the top of the jar. Staring at it in amazement she said to herself "what will they think of next?"

As they rode into the fair grounds, Susanna requested "William, please stop by the baking tent so that I can unload these pies and get them in a good location so the judges can admire them." "I'll need both of you to help me place them on the tables."

Greeting the other wives beginning to show up at the tent at the about the same time as the Elliotts did, Susanna went about arranging the pies in a neat order, not necessarily the first in line to be judged, but somewhere near the middle so the judges would have had some examples first before they began judging her pies. This strategy had worked well last year at the fair when her wild plum pies won the blue ribbon for best all around pie in the county.

"I'm off to the shooting range" Luke joyfully said as he gathered up his powder horn, ammunition, and long rifle and started to leave for the remote area where the shots would not endanger anyone nearby.

"Good luck, son" Susanna said bussing him on the cheek before he left. "Don't forget to keep your powder dry" William jokingly added remembering how disappointed Luke was last year when it really got wet from the sprinkling rain. He patted Luke on the top of his head for good luck and added "Goodness, you're getting tall."

Arriving at the shooting range, Luke found a comfortable spot for the competition and began to load the long rifle. First, placing the rifle butt on the ground, Luke measured out just the right amount of black powder from the horn and poured it down the barrel of the rifle. Then he took a small patch of cloth salvaged from one of Susanna's old skirts that had been torn badly one day when she was out picking blackberries along the creek. Placing the patch, which had been greased with a little fat on the top of the barrel, Luke set the small lead ball on top of it and using the attached ramrod, shoved it down into the barrel so that it was packed snugly against the black powder. Now, all was ready to aim and fire with exception of the last very important step, and that was to pour another small amount of black powder from the horn into the pan just under the hammer which was then covered by another metal piece of the rifle. When this metal was struck by the flint in the falling hammer, sparks flew igniting the powder in the pan which, in turn, would cause the powder in the barrel to explode sending the lead ball on its way to the target.

The Kentucky rifle was a good five feet long from one end to the other and Luke could easily load it while sitting on his horse and placing the butt all the way down on the ground. Today, he stood upon an oak tree stump, which gave him easy loading access to the barrel.

Carefully placing the long rifle in the fork of a nearby tree, Luke took steady aim at a gourd that had been set up some hundred yards away to be used as targets. Taking a deep breath and holding it for a few seconds, he gently squeezed the trigger which released the hammer and flint, striking the metal plate, igniting the powder in the pan, and exploding the powder in the barrel sending the lead ball hurtling towards the gourd target. Luke was used to the kick the rifle produced after each firing, but it still gave him a good wallop each time he fired it.

The smoke from the barrel cleared just in time for Luke to see the gourd splatter when the ball hit it dead center.

"What a shot!" a voice behind him commented in that beautiful southern softness that Luke longed to hear. "You're really good with that rifle and I'd like to see you do it again" Elizabeth said walking up to Luke's side and patting him on the back.

Her touch caused his heart to beat just a little faster as he turned to look into her deep blue eyes once again. "Hi, Elizabeth. Didn't hear you come up behind me" Luke spoke lowering his rifle.

"I didn't want to spoil your aim, but I was watching you load that long rifle up on that stump. As tall as you are you still need a ladder, don't you?" she laughed.

Luke, anxious to show Elizabeth he could smack another of the gourds which had been placed another twenty yards beyond the first one he had obliterated with his first shot, took careful aim again and repeated the ritual of firing the rifle. Again, the second gourd was blasted into a hundred pieces with the well placed ball.

"That's enough for now" Luke said placing the leather cover over the rifle and cradling it in his arms. "Lets go see what all is going on at the fair".

Spending the better part of the day just wandering around and looking at all of the exhibits that the ranchers and farmers had brought in and sampling some of the foods that were being offered kept Luke and Elizabeth entertained until it was time for the turkey shoot.

A loud voice from a short man standing on a small platform announced to all that the shoot was about to start at the range and all were invited to come to watch.

Luke picked up his rifle and ammunition from the parked wagon where he had placed it earlier and the two of them headed down the path where the competition was shortly to begin.

"Gosh" Luke exclaimed. "I didn't know so many people were going to be shooting today" when he looked at the line of over twenty men readying their rifles. "I don't know if I can beat these fellows or not."

Taking his assigned place on the firing range, Luke began the procedure of loading the rifle again and used an overturned bucket to stand on this time so that he could pour the powder down the barrel easily. Then Luke remembered the prize to be given for the best shot…..the Colt pistol, and he gritted his teeth in determination that he was going to give this chance his best.

The gourds had all been placed at fifty yards for the first shot. Those failing to shatter them were automatically disqualified and would have to wait until next year to compete again. "Good luck" Elizabeth whispered to Luke as he readied his rifle. That was all he needed to shake the jitters from him and restore his confidence in his shooting ability. Squeezing the trigger as he had done so many times before, the ball found its mark in the first gourd with virtually no effort at all, splattering it as the others had done earlier during the practice rounds. "Good for you, Luke" Elizabeth spoke proudly.

Of the twenty two original shooters, seven had missed the easy target which left fifteen reloading and preparing to shoot at the targets which had been moved to a hundred yards down the range. Repeating the oft-practiced method of easy squeezing, Luke took his deep breath and fired once again.

A roar of applause erupted from behind the firing line as the smoke from the rifles cleared revealing only six gourds that had been hit. Luke's was no where to be seen which meant that he would advance to the next firing with five of the older men who had been firing their rifles longer than Luke had been alive.

"I'm awfully nervous" Luke told Elizabeth as he spilled some powder on the ground. Elizabeth walked to Luke and whispered into his ear "you've done this before and I know you can do it again easily." Grabbing on to his free arm, Elizabeth gave him a squeeze of admiration which caused Luke to realize all he had to do was aim this rifle one more time.

Six rifles rang out with shots aimed at the six gourds that had been advanced another fifty yards to one hundred fifty, almost the maximum range of the Kentucky rifles. Three remained, but Luke's was gone!

A hundred fifty yards, the crowd yelled in excitement marveling at the accuracy of the three remaining shooters. The other two were bearded men who obviously had spent a lot of time in the wild as hunters or maybe even fighters in the army. And here was Luke, with just a few whiskers growing on his chin! The last three wished each other luck as they reloaded and prepared to fire at the gourds marked at a distance of an unbelievable two hundred yards this time.

Once again, Elizabeth gave Luke the confidence he needed for this last shot by placing her hand on his and giving it a gentle squeeze. Luke's mind was reeling as he drew a bead on the gourd that was hardly visible at this distance knowing that only once before had he hit a target so far away and that was after five or six attempts. Now, here he was with one last shot between him, the blue ribbon and the pistol, which would be awarded to the one who could smash that gourd in the distance.

Kablaam! Kablaam! Kablaam! The three shots rang out as the crowd once again roared its admiration for the shooters. Luke had closed his eyes after the shot and was afraid to open them to see just how far he had missed the gourd. The crowd was going wild with cheers when Luke finally opened them to see two gourds still down the range. His was gone! He had bested the two veteran shooters with his marksmanship and had sent his gourd tumbling off in the distance splattering it into a hundred pieces.

As he lowered his rifle, Elizabeth ran up to him, threw her arms around his neck, and kissed him on the cheek. "I knew you could do it, cowboy!" she exclaimed. Luke could hardly contain himself and wrapping his free arm around Elizabeth told her softly "thanks for being here."

Stepping up to the platform as the proud winner of the turkey shoot, Luke accepts the blue ribbon for having outshot some of the best riflemen in central Texas. Not only did he win the ribbon, but the fair committee now announced that a special additional award was to be given.

"For your expert marksmanship and winning today's contest, we would like you to have this additional prize, a brand new Cold Navy Revolver" the judge exclaimed to the crowd and to Luke. Beaming with pride, Luke accepted the double award and could hardly wait to share the good fortune with Elizabeth who was waiting patiently for him at the bottom of the platform stairs.

They both hurried off to see their parents to show them Luke's Blue Ribbon and Colt Revolver.

Dusk was beginning to cast its long shadows across the fair grounds and from the pavilion in the middle of the area came the first bars of music from the local brass band. To call it music was somewhat of a misconception because the band was made up of folks who had been playing their cornets and trombones occasionally whenever they could get together as a group. They were trying their best and somehow the flat notes didn't really matter to anyone because everyone was enjoying the end of the day's festivities.

Luke and Elizabeth sat by an oak tree listening to the music and getting to know each other better bit by bit. They told each other stories of how they had grown up, Luke on the Running E, and Elizabeth first on the Mississippi farm and now at their ranch, the Circle Bar W.

William came looking for Luke saying they needed to head back to the ranch shortly so that they could get there at a decent hour. Knowing that the ride back would take another hour, Luke prepared to stand up, but Elizabeth grabbed his hand and pulled him back down again.

"I have enjoyed this day so very much that I can hardly wait until I see you again, maybe next weekend if you could come up. We'll have that picnic I promised you down by the creek if you like" Elizabeth said in her best Mississippi drawl.

"Elizabeth, I, too, can hardly…." Luke attempted to answer, but Elizabeth leaned forward and kissed him gently before he could say a single word.

"Does that mean you'll come?" Elizabeth asked.

Luke, gathering his wits about him knowing that he again was blushing a beet red, but glad Elizabeth couldn't see in the shadows. "I'll come Saturday morning and spend the whole day with you" Luke answered quickly.

"Tell you what" Elizabeth added. "Plan to stay over Saturday night, you can have the extra bedroom, and we can go to church on Sunday morning in Salem."

Luke wasn't sure about going to church because there hadn't been much time to make the ride into Salem on Sundays in the past, but the opportunity to spend two whole days with Elizabeth was almost more than he could ask for and going to church might just be all right after all.

Walking hand in hand back to join the Wyatts at their wagon as they prepared to make their own ride back to their ranch, Luke bid them all a good night and winked at Elizabeth. "Hope your folks won't mind having company next weekend."

"They'll love it" Elizabeth reassured Luke as he helped her up into their wagon. "I'll see you Saturday, and bring that rifle and new pistol with you. I'd like to learn how to shoot them."

By now, Luke felt as if he were two feet off the ground and he sauntered back to join his family already aboard their wagon. "We'd better get going now so we can get home before midnight" William mentioned.

"Look what I have" Susanna said to Luke as she reached into her bag pulling out a shiny blue ribbon. "Won the pie contest again this year."

"I'm so proud of you, Mama, and now we can hang two blue ribbons up on the wall, one for you and one for me" Luke said.

The moon rose higher into the jet black night as Luke settled down in the wagon on his elbows thinking of the wonders of the day and especially of his spending it with Elizabeth. "Next week, I'll be with the Wyatts" Luke thought as he watched the moon play hide and seek with the clouds. "Next week I am in Heaven!"

"I heard today that things are brewing in Washington, D.C. that might affect us here in Texas" William mentioned to Susanna.

"Like what?" Susanna asked.

"Don't think it will bother us at the ranch too much, but folks around are buzzing about the fact that slavery may be done away with and that it will mean the loss of the Negroes they have" William added. "I never believed in slavery as you know, but most folks need theirs to keep the farms and ranches in business.

"How will that affect Micah, Lucy, and Joshua?" Susanna questioned.

"Probably not very much since my father emancipated them in Virginia long before we came here. They've been a part of our family as you know for a long time and they know they are free people and belong to no one but themselves, but the other ranchers are going to argue that no Washington bureaucrat is going to tell them what they can and can't do with their slaves and property. You know, they consider them as their property bought and sold all legal like" William answered.

"Talk like that can ruin a country" Susanna observed as they turned into the road leading up to the ranch.

Chapter Seven
A Deadly Shot

The next Saturday morning, Luke awoke rather early with anticipation of meeting Elizabeth for the picnic she had planned for them at the Circle Bar W. He stumbled out of bed, bathed, shaved his few chin whiskers as carefully as he could with his straight razor that had belonged to his Papa when he was Luke's age, and put on clean pants and shirt before heading out to the kitchen where Susanna was already preparing breakfast of eggs and bacon for him. Luke had been smelling the wonderful aroma of bacon before he even got out of bed and he was looking forward to several pieces before heading northward to Elizabeth.

The sun was just beginning to come up over the mesquite trees in the east pasture when Luke headed out to the stable to saddle up Golden for the ride to the Wyatt's. Patting Golden on her neck and rubbing her forehead, he gently placed the saddle blanket on her back and then reached for the saddle sitting on the upper rail of the stall. With a hefty swing, the saddle was lifted up and over Golden with a minimum of effort. Going about securing the saddle properly, Luke chuckled when he thought of how he and Joshua used to have to work as a team in order to get the heavy saddle in place. Climbing astride his horse, Luke reached for the Kentucky rifle leaning up against the side of the stall and put it in front of him as he rode out of the stable. He checked his new Colt Revolver now strapped to his right hip and hoped that Elizabeth would like learning to fire it later on that day.

Passing by Joshua's cabin on the way out, Luke stopped to visit his dear friend who was out gathering firewood for the stove so that his mother could start his breakfast. Joshua could tell that Luke was in a good mood when he had heard him whistling earlier in the stable.

"You still have a hard time carrying a tune," Joshua chided Luke, "but I did sorta recognize what you were trying to whistle. Where you headin' out to so early in the morning? Goin' fishing without me?"

"No," Luke replied. "I'm on my way to absolute heaven for the weekend and will surely find an angel there waiting for me to arrive" he grinned. "The Wyatts have invited me up for a visit and I'm on my way up there."

"See you when you get back" Joshua shouted to Luke as he headed down the path towards the north pasture. Joshua watched Luke for a short while and began to realize he was going to be playing second fiddle from now on since Luke had found him someone new to devote his attention towards.

As the sun rose higher and the time approached ten o'clock, Luke made his way across the north pasture and noticed that Golden was acting a little strange. She was beginning to shy occasionally and would miss a step causing her to change her trot. Luke sensing that something was wrong pulled the reins and stopped Golden dead in her tracks and stood up in the stirrups trying to make out the brown object lying on the ground a couple hundred feet away.

"It's a dead steer" Luke said out loud as if someone could hear him.

Approaching the carcass, he realized that the animal had been freshly killed, but whatever had done so was gone from sight. Studying it some more, Luke realized that the signs of the kill were obviously from a cougar, probably the same one that had been marauding the herds of not only the Running E, but also the adjoining ranches. This was not the first one that had been killed here because two others had been found last week. Searching the surrounding countryside, Luke tried to spot where the cougar could have gone, but saw nothing.

Luke put his foot in the stirrup and as he was lifting himself up he checked his Kentucky rifle and his Colt at his hip just to be on the safe side.

He should have checked the oak tree just ahead of him to notice that the cougar had taken refuge on one of the branches that hung directly over the path Luke was taking.

Golden, upon nearing the underside of the tree, reared up on her back legs and caused Luke to tumble backwards out of the saddle and land hard on the ground. Stunned, Luke quickly regained his senses and realized what had caused her to rear up like that when he spotted the cougar ready to pounce on him and his horse. Unable to reach his Kentucky rifle on the ground a few feet away in time, Luke pulled the Colt from its holster and fired three shots directly at the attacker before it hit the ground dead.

"I can't believe what just happened" Luke thought to himself as he checked the dead animal, which lay before him. "My new gun saved our lives. Well, I can now tell Papa when I get back that we won't have to worry any more about this killer doing any more harm to our cattle or to the other ranchers either."

Taking his hunting knife from its sheath, Luke very triumphantly cuts an ear from the cougar, wipes off the excess blood from it on the grass, and puts it into his saddle bag as a trophy and proof that he had indeed done away with this nuisance. Normally, cougars will stay away from humans, but this one was an exception and it paid with its life.

Gathering his wits together, Luke calls to Golden who had wandered off just a few feet from where the cougar lay, but refused to come any closer because of the smell of the animal. Stepping up to her, Luke gently calms her down and remounts, looking back at the scene and thinking he was really a very lucky person. He patted Golden on the neck and thanked her for her warning.

As he approached the Wyatt's ranch house, Elizabeth was already on the porch waiting for him. Luke's heart leaped to his throat in anticipation of seeing her once again.

"What on earth happened to you?" Elizabeth asked quizzingly.

"Had a little run in with that cougar that's been bothering the cattle for the last couple of weeks" Luke offered. Patting his new Colt on his hip he boasted "works well. Fired three shots at him as he jumped from the tree we were just going under and killed him before he hit the ground."

Elizabeth was all atwitter at the news, but took Luke by the hand and brought him inside to settle him down for a bit.

Mrs. Wyatt had just put on a fresh pot of coffee and the aroma wafted about the house. Luke hadn't developed much of a taste for coffee, but it was time for him to learn more of its appeal and he readily accepted the cup that she offered to him.

"Tell me more about that cougar" Mr. Wyatt said. "We lost a calf a couple of weeks ago down close to your north pasture and I'll bet that was the same cougar that got it then."

"It won't be bothering us any more," Luke proudly said and pulled the ear out of his saddle bag to show him what he had done.

"Enough of this talk about dead cows" Elizabeth interrupted. "Come on, Luke, show me that new pistol and I want to shoot your Kentucky rifle out by the oak tree. Mother has fixed us a picnic lunch for later and we'll have that by the creek."

Luke set up a couple of rocks on the top rail of the fence about a hundred feet away and found a vee in the oak tree to rest the barrel of the gun on as he took aim. Splattering the rock into several pieces, Luke showed Elizabeth how to reload and placed the rifle in the vee once again.

"Now let me show you how it's done" Luke said as Elizabeth took up the position to fire. "This thing has a powerful kick to it so be prepared for its reaction."

Standing behind her with his left arm steadying her left arm and his right hand placed gently on her right hand, Elizabeth took aim at one of the other rocks on the rail and squeezed the trigger. The kick caught her off guard somewhat and she was pushed back into Luke rather suddenly. Luke, realizing he had his arms now tightly around her, he called her attention to the missing rock on the rail and kissed her on her cheek.

"Lookit what you just did" he proudly boasted to Elizabeth. "You blasted that rock into a dozen pieces on your very first shot. Whatta shooter you are. Are you sure you haven't done this before?"

Elizabeth turned and faced Luke beaming with her accomplishment and Luke nearly buckled at the knees when he looked into her deep blue eyes once again.

"Thanks for showing me, Luke" Elizabeth said starring back into Luke's eyes. "Now show me how that new Colt works."

They both knew then that this relationship was going to develop into a deep and lasting one as they later walked arm in arm back to the house.

"It's time for a picnic and I'm hungry" Elizabeth exclaimed as they walked up the front porch stairs. My mother has fixed us some delicious fried chicken and some more of that gingerbread that you liked so well."

"I'm hungry too" Luke admitted.

The rest of the afternoon was spent under the oak tree down at the creek as Luke and Elizabeth talked of many things and getting to know each other better and better with each hour. By the time Sunday afternoon rolled around and time for Luke to return to the Running W, Elizabeth walked to the corral with Luke and helped him saddle up Golden.

Tightening the cinch on the saddle, Luke turned to Elizabeth to tell her that this had been the most wonderful weekend he had ever spent and she responded by standing on the tiptoes and kissing him gently. "It's been the most fantastic time I have ever had" she added.

Taking the blue ribbon that had been holding her black hair in place, Elizabeth handed it to Luke and said, "this is just something to remember me by."

Luke stammered and collected his senses once again trying to think of something to give to her when he reached into the saddlebag and pulled out the now drying cougar's ear. Elizabeth laughed and told him she surely would be reminded of him each time she saw this trophy.

Chapter Eight

Angry Discussions

The fall and winter of 1859 crept into Texas with the changing of the leaves, blustery northers, and eventual snow, which dusted the hill country once again. Then it quietly moved on to herald the arrival of spring of 1860 when the bluebonnets began to bloom in profusion almost as far as the eye could see.

Elizabeth and Luke had become another year older and continued to see each other virtually every weekend. Occasionally, when Luke was working the north pasture, she would come racing up on her horse to see him and to bring him a picnic lunch which they would enjoy under one of the big oak trees. Turns out, Elizabeth was an excellent horsewoman and loved to challenge Luke to races down to the creek and back. They both had finished their schooling, which gave them more time for ranch duties.

Elizabeth's life was now centered around Luke and between them they both knew that someday they probably would be married at the Methodist church in Salem where they were now seen every Sunday morning sitting in the back pew dressed in their finest.

Joshua and Luke continued to be very strong friends, but Joshua admitted that he didn't get to see Luke as much as he did when they were younger and sometimes felt a little jealous of Elizabeth and her devotion to Luke.

However, in the late afternoons, the two young men would often grab their fishing gear and head for the river and its never-ending supply of trout and catfish.

"Guess we'd better be heading back…..the sun's beginning to set and I know supper will be ready when we get there" Luke declared.

"Yep. Got a good line of trout this time, didn't we?" Joshua stated. "I'll carry the fish if you'll carry the poles."

Reaching to pick up the gunny sack loaded with the fish, Joshua didn't hear the buzz in time to avoid the rattlesnake coiled up under the tree when it lunged its ugly head towards him and struck his outreached hand, burying its fangs deep into the flesh near his right thumb.

Reeling back in horror, Joshua screams to Luke "I'm bit! That rattler bit me on my hand!"

Luke, having seen a snakebite before knew what he had to do to save his terrified friend an agonizing sickness and possible death. Quickly reaching for his knife in the sheath on his belt, he stuck the blade in the still smoldering campfire to sterilize it as much as possible. Luke pushed the frantic Joshua down on the ground to keep him from thrashing around which would cause the snake venom to spread rapidly through his veins. Taking the hot blade, he cut two small gashes over the penetration holes where the rattler had injected its poison and began sucking out the blood, spitting it and the venom behind him on the ground.

By this time, Joshua was beginning to feel faint and Luke had to keep him from slipping off to unconsciousness by smacking him in the face now and then with a gentle slap. Taking his own belt, he wrapped it around Joshua's right arm below the elbow and tied it off to form a tourniquet. Standing him upright, they headed for their horses just a few steps away where they were fastened to a mesquite branch. Joshua began to moan "I'm so sick. I'm so sick. Please get me home before I pass out Luke."

"You're gonna have to help me a little, Joshua" Luke spoke sternly, "and put your foot up in the stirrup." Getting him that far enabled Luke to push him on up onto the saddle telling him to hold on to the saddle horn and not to let go. Jumping astride Golden in two quick movements, Luke took the reins to Apple and headed them both quickly back to the ranch house only about a mile away.

By the time they got within shouting distance of the house, Luke began calling to his father to come help him. Hearing the distressed voice, William jumps up from his desk and races outside to find Luke taking a limp Joshua off of his saddle.

"Snake bit!" Luke tells William. "I lanced the bite and put the tourniquet on just like I saw you do once on one of the cattle drives when that drover got bit that time" Luke excitedly exclaimed.

Looking at the wound on Joshua's hand William told Luke "you did well. Let's get him inside and you go fetch Micah and Lucy and tell them to get here quick" William directed.

The two of them, carrying Joshua who by this time had lapsed into unconsciousness, placed him on a bed in the spare bedroom. Susanna came running in to see what had happened and stopped dead in her tracks when she saw Joshua's arm hanging limp from the side of the bed.

"What happened" Susanna asked.

"He was reaching for the gunny sack of fish and didn't see the rattler before it struck him" Luke explained. "I lanced it and put that tourniquet on him before we came home."

Luke made a mad dash to get Micah and Lucy at their home, knocked on the door loudly, and burst in. "Joshua's been snake bit and I brought him up to the house and Mama and Papa are taking care of him right now."

The three of them hurried back to the house and Lucy kneeled down to inspect the wound in Joshua's hand. Then, looking up at Luke said "he'll live. He's gonna be a little sick for a couple of days, but he'll live all right."

"Just the same," William says, "first thing in the morning I'll drive him in to Salem to see Doc Calley."

It was long after midnight when Joshua began to come around and wondered where he was. Lucy and Micah were at his bedside to reassure him that he was now in good hands, but had given everyone a good scare.

"Where's Luke?" Joshua quietly asked.

"Sent him off to bed already. He did a fine job of taking care of you and Mr. Elliott is going to drive you into Salem tomorrow morning so Doc Calley can take a look at your hand. Right now, you go on back to sleep" Lucy said patting him on the forehead.

"Luke's my friend, my very good friend" Joshua murmured as he drifted off to sleep.

The next morning, William was up very early and Luke was not far behind him stumbling out of bed and dressing. After a quick breakfast of coffee and pancakes that Susanna had prepared for them, they hitched the wagon and placed several blankets in the back of it so that Joshua could ride in reasonable comfort.

Helping Joshua into the wagon, Lucy climbed into it and sat down beside him for the ride into Salem to see Doc Calley. William drove and Luke rode on the buckboard beside him as they headed down the road.

Entering Salem shortly after daybreak, the wagon pulled up to the doctor's office and Luke went in to explain to him what had happened to Joshua the night before.

"Another snakebite" Doc Calley lamented. "It's about the seventh or eighth I've had just this month. Guess those snakes are getting restless and have nothing better to do than give people a bad time" he added jokingly. "Haven't lost a patient yet, though."

Taking a look at Joshua's swelling hand, Doc Calley studied it carefully and examined his arm from his fingers to his shoulder. "Who did the original lancing of the bite?" he asked.

"I did" Luke answered. "I had seen Papa do it before on a cattle drive and I knew I had to act quick before that venom spread."

"You probably saved his life" he commented to Luke. "I've seen young men come in here with snakebites that hadn't been treated like you did for Joshua and they almost lost their arms or legs depending on where they were bitten. A couple of them almost died."

After Joshua's hand was bandaged and his arm placed in a sling, Doc Calley gave Lucy some medicine for him to take until it healed and advised her to check back with him the next week just to see if things were progressing satisfactorily.

Climbing gingerly aboard the wagon with Luke giving him a lift up, Joshua smiled at the doctor and muttered a "thank you" for taking good care of him.

"You're welcome, Joshua, but the credit really goes to Luke because of his quick action after that snake got a hold of you" Doc Calley called to them as they drove off toward town.

As the wagon passed the front of the General Store, Luke heard a couple of the town ruffians sitting on the porch with their boots up on the rail make a comment that it looked like someone was on the way to the market to be sold. Luke wheeled himself around and stared at them as they grinned through their ugly broken teeth, but said nothing. He had hoped that Joshua and Lucy hadn't heard the comment, but he knew that they had from the hurt look in Lucy's eyes.

Mr. Stuard, who had been sweeping the front porch when the wagon passed, had heard the comments from the two misfits and told them to get up and leave his porch and not to return. The two knew better than to mess with him, standing there in his long white apron and rather formidable looking broom, because they had heard he could handle almost any situation with a swiftness that legends are made of. The skedaddled and didn't look back.

The ride back was mostly in silence. William whispered to Luke that it looked as if Abe Lincoln was going to be elected next year and if he were elected he would set all the Negroes free from slavery, which surely would lead to terrible happenings in the south.

William dreaded the thought that Texas would follow whatever the rest of the southern states would do if the northerners forced their beliefs on them and did, in fact, send in federal troops to enforce whatever those in Washington, D.C. imposed. This was something that he just could not tolerate and was surprised to learn that Luke felt the same way that he did.

Texas was very dear to the Elliotts and they believed that they would do whatever was necessary to ensure the state's security and would protect their way of life at whatever cost was necessary.

The following week, Luke and William had heard that a town meeting was to be held in Salem and lawmakers from Austin were to be there to talk to the local people about the decisions facing Texas in the very near future. Saddling their horses, they rode into town on Saturday to attend the meeting.

The building where the gathering was to take place was packed and ranchers and farmers from all over the area were there to express their views angrily about their property and how they were going to keep their Negroes regardless of what Washington might have to say.

The agreement among those there was almost unanimous that they believed Texas should stand up to the federal government and tell them that Texas wanted no part in the abolishment of the slave issue. Leave the state alone was the consensus of opinions and the anger of those present spread rapidly throughout the meeting.

William and Luke returned to the ranch late that afternoon knowing that Texas was in trouble and that it probably would follow the lead of the rest of the southern states, some of which were already talking of seceding from the union that was not yet a hundred years old.

Susanna called to the two men as they rode up to the barn and they turned towards her before dismounting. "The sickness has come to a couple of the ranches out to the west and the rumor is that two have already died from it" she said in a worried tone of voice. I think I may need to head out there in the morning to see if I can be of any assistance to those who are sick. From what a rider passing by said this afternoon while you all were at the meeting was that those that had died were children, but it was spreading almost too fast for them to stop it."

Luke hitched the wagon up the next morning and climbed aboard to drive it back to the ranch house to pick up Susanna. "You're not going, Luke" she said. "I don't want you to come down with the sickness, too."

"Mama." Luke spoke defiantly. "You need my help and I am going if for no other reason to drive you there and back."

Susanna, knowing that to argue the point with Luke was fruitless, agreed that they both would stay only for the day and do whatever they could in the time they were there. Driving down the road, Doc Calley approached them in his wagon heading in the same direction towards the other ranches as well. He was glad to see Luke and Susanna, but warned them of the dangers of being around those who were sick.

The first ranch that the trio came to was not suffering from the sickness, but he advised them that the adjoining ranch had two people sick and probably needed some attention. Arriving there about a half hour later, Doc Calley examined an older boy and the wife of the rancher. Staying with them for about an hour, he came out and began to wash his hands in the bowl on the washstand. A worried look from him as he approached Susanna and Luke told them that the matter was extremely serious. Whispering aside to Susanna, he said to her one dreaded word….."diptheria!"

Most of the ranches the trio visited were free of the sickness, but all were warned to boil all of their drinking water and to wash all of their eating utensils with hot water and lye soap to help prevent the spread. Those ranches that had the sickness were quarantined with the same warnings.

The last ranch they visited had an infant that was almost lifeless, but still managing to breathe laboriously from the sickness that affected the throat and lungs. The mother was sick in the bedroom and Doc Calley and Susanna both went in to see about her. He handed Luke the infant to hold while they were busy with the mother and he went out and sat down on the porch, cradling the infant in his arms as he looked upon its tiny face. After an hour or so, Luke realized the infant was no longer moving and a feeling of horror fell all over him like a storm spreading from the hills onto the pasture below.

Still holding the lifeless infant, Luke looked at Doc Calley and Susanna when they came out of the bedroom with a feeling of disbelief. Just how could something so tiny be snatched away so soon, he wondered. Susanna took the baby from Luke's arms and wrapped it in the tiny blanket she pulled from its cradle. Placing the infant in the cradle, she looked upon the tearful face of the rancher whose whole life was crumbling about him as he saw his wife deathly ill and his infant already gone from the sickness.

Back home at the ranch, Luke and Susanna rolled up to the barn just before sundown and Luke went about unhitching the wagon and placing the horse in its stall for the evening. Susanna had already gone into the house and was explaining to William about the diptheria at the next ranches when Luke came in. "I'm heading on up to the Wyatts just to check on them and to make sure they get the information about what's going on west of here" he told them. "I may stay up there for the night, but I'll be back as soon as I can in the morning" he explained as he grabbed his pistol and a piece of bread to munch on as he rode north.

Luke made the trip to the Wyatts and Elizabeth in about an hour and tied his horse's reins to the post by the front steps. She had heard him ride up and met him at the front door wondering just why he was coming up here so late in the evening. Explaining to the Wyatts of the events of the day, he was glad to learn that none of the ranch hands at the Circle Bar W were sick and especially that Elizabeth was all right, too.

After the Wyatts had offered Luke something to eat and drink, they excused themselves and told Luke just to stay on overnight so that he wouldn't have to make the trip back home in the dark. Luke was thankful for the offer and gladly accepted them, bidding them a good night as they left the living room for bed.

Walking out in the moonlit front yard later with Elizabeth, Luke was just beginning to unwind from all the worries he had faced during the day. He spoke of the diptheria and how deadly it could be if the people don't take precautions. He talked again of the infant dying in his arms and how he couldn't understand why something so innocent had to pay such a price. He spoke of the town meeting he and Papa had attended and shared his feelings for Texas and how he was prepared to stand by his homeland at any cost. He talked of the comments made in Salem about Lucy and Joshua and described to her how he had almost lost his best friend to a rattlesnake bite.

As he poured his heart out to Elizabeth, Luke explained to her that he was deeply in love with her and that he couldn't think of spending the rest of his life without her by his side. Mustering up all the remaining bit of courage he could pull from his tired inner self, Luke looked into Elizabeth's face with the moon shining brightly on it and said to her "Elizabeth, I'd like to ask your father for your hand in marriage…..if that's all right with you!"

"Luke Elliott" Elizabeth beamed with a tear of joy running down her cheek, "I've been waiting so long for you to ask me that very question. You know I love you and I think I've loved you since that first day when I saw you riding your horse in your altogether after chasing that fox and I, too, cannot think of the rest of my life without you with me and I know already what my father will say because I've already told him that I was going to marry you and he and my mother both agreed that they loved you too and that they thought my decision was a wonderful one. So there! Does that answer your question?" having spoken every word in one long breath. Standing on her tiptoes she gave him a long kiss.

The moon again shown brightly after it had come from behind a cloud for a while. Luke and Elizabeth stood in the shadows, his arm around her waist, both of them not saying a thing, but just savoring the moment as one that they would cherish for the rest of their lives together.

Chapter Nine
War Clouds

William and Luke climbed the icy steps to the capitol building in Austin where they were seeking a visit with Sam Houston, now the Governor of Texas, the only man ever to have been elected as governor of two separate states, Tennessee and now Texas. They had ridden in from the ranch after Christmas 1860 to seek information from William's old commander and wanted to hear from Houston first hand just what his thoughts were for Texas' future if the state should decide to secede from the Union.

Houston was a slave owner and a staunch opponent of abolition, but a strong supporter of the Union and feared that if Texas did secede he would not be able to serve as governor because of the political upheaval it would cause.

Entering the outer office of the governor, William spoke to the secretary sitting behind a large desk piled high with papers of importance for one cause or another.

"May I help you?" the man asked, looking up and over his glasses that had slipped down his nose.

"I am William Elliott from Salem and my son and I would like to visit with General Houston to discuss the problems of secession and how it will affect Texas" he replied.

"I'm terribly sorry, but Governor Houston is much to busy to visit with anyone at this time, but….." and before he could finish his sentence a loud booming voice came from the next office and interrupted the secretary.

"Is that the man who captured Santa Anna single handedly standing out there?" Houston roared as he appeared in his doorway, his head almost touching the top of the opening, and with a big grin offered an outstretched hand of welcome. "Come on in here and have a seat." Leaving the secretary with his mouth agape, William and Luke entered and took a seat upon the governor's big leather couch.

"I haven't seen you since San Jacinto, but I've heard about you and that excellent ranch you have out in Salem. Is this your son?" Houston asked.

"Good afternoon, general, this is my son, Luke" William said proudly as Luke rose and shook the governor's hand.

"I'm mighty proud to know you, Governor Houston" Luke responded.

Spending well over an hour with the governor was far more than they had imagined, but the conversation went from happy reunion to talk of secession and war with the north. Houston explained to them that if the south were to go to war with the north it would destroy the nation as they knew it and the rebuilding would take decades afterwards. He knew that the north had more men for the army and more money to provide for their needs than the south could ever hope to put together. He believed, however, that war was inevitable because the way of life in the south and in Texas was about to be tested. He also knew that with Lincoln being elected president that the first thing that he probably would do would be to emancipate all the slaves throughout the nation.

Saying their goodbyes to the governor, William and Luke walked sadly down to the livery stable where they had placed their horses earlier. Saddling up, they dreaded the long ride back to the ranch, but knew that Susanna would have dinner waiting for them and that kept them moving at a brisk pace all the way home.

The new year of 1861 arrived at the ranches with another cold norther blowing down through the flatlands of central Texas bringing with it miserably cold rain and cloudy skies that spread to the horizon for days on end. Luke and Elizabeth celebrated the holiday with a gathering of both families at the Running E and lots of delicious food served from a long table in the dining room.

Talk of Texas' secession weighed heavily on everyone at the dinner and Susanna, Jane, and Elizabeth excused themselves afterwards so that the men folk could discuss politics and the fate of Texas in the future. Luke could hardly wait to get this discussion over with so that he and Elizabeth could talk about their plans for the wedding sometime in the coming months. They both had wanted to make it an April wedding because the weather would be nicer by then and the bluebonnets would be in full bloom once again. Little did they know that everything would be put on hold because of the events that were about to happen in the south and especially in Texas.

Lincoln had, in fact, been elected to the presidency and the south was boiling mad. Secession talk was in full force and in February Texas joined several other states in their threat of secession from the Union. War was now imminent and there was nothing much the south could do about it any more but to form their own union of states.

Texas seceded from the Union on February 1, 1861.

Sam Houston was adamant in his refusal to swear allegiance to the new Confederate States of America and called the secession of Texas from the Union illegal. The Texas legislature upheld the secession and forced Houston who had been the governor of Tennessee before coming to Texas, the general that led Texas to its independence, the president of the new Republic of Texas, and now governor of the state of Texas to step down from office, replacing him with another who was more sympathetic to the southern cause. Houston sadly moved his family to Huntsville where he remained throughout the war, but not living long enough to see it end.
In April, William came riding up the ranch at full gallop having been in Austin for three days and bounded into the living room expecting to

see Susanna, but was met by Luke instead. "The southern troops have fired on Fort Sumter in South Carolina and war has been declared!" he excitedly said to him.

"Papa", Luke quietly said. "When you were in Austin, Mama took sick. Joshua went in to Salem to get Doc Calley who is on his way here now and should be here shortly."

William quietly entered the bedroom, saw Susanna on the bed, and raced to her side to ask her what was the matter. "I don't know" Susanna answered, "but I'm really very, very sick. I'm having trouble breathing and can't keep any food or water down because it just comes right back up when I try."

Doc Calley gently closed the bedroom door and came to William and Luke standing in the living room with uneasy apprehension. "Diphtheria, William. She has diphtheria" he said in a quiet voice.

****

April, which was supposed to bring happiness to the Elliott family with the wedding of Luke and Elizabeth had now been replaced by the untimely passing of Susanna Elliott from the dreaded disease that usually struck small children, but in this case had claimed this beautiful frontier woman who had withstood the trials of moving to a new land and clawing out a thriving ranch with her devoted husband and son.

The April rain poured heavily on the small hill near the north pasture of the Running E where local townsfolk had gathered to pay their last respects to the cheerful mother who had helped most of them in one way or another for the last many years when they needed care themselves. The minister from the Methodist church in Salem spoke to the crowd and to William and Luke with the usual messages of condolences for Susanna's passing.

William stood alongside Luke and Elizabeth who held Luke's hand for these last moments with his mother as the small pine box was lowered into the grave by Micah and several of the ranch hands. Joshua stood nearby with rain dripping down from his hat remembering the wonderful times he had spent with Susanna in the kitchen at night when she taught him how to read and write and love poetry.

Later, at the ranch house, Elizabeth poured William and Luke a cup of coffee and they all sat together trying to smile and hoping to get through the next few days with a minimum of sorrow.

Chapter Ten

A Difference of Opinion

The secession of South Carolina led six other states to join it in the rebellion against the northern way of thinking. Mississippi, Florida, Alabama, Georgia, Louisiana, and Texas realized that the southern way of life was being challenged with regard to slavery and convinced Virginia, Arkansas, and Tennessee to join with them. In February of 1861, the Confederate Constitution was drawn up claiming the autonomy of the states involved and selected Jefferson Davis as the President of the Confederacy.

Lincoln, after being inaugurated as president in March, openly declared that he had absolutely no reason or plans to end slavery in the states where it already existed including those in the north. He had wanted to solve the issue of slavery through diplomacy, but was totally unwilling to accept secession and would not tolerate the thought of breaking up the union. His thoughts about slavery would soon change.

April of that year had witnessed the capture of Fort Sumter in South Carolina. The union garrison stationed there was is desperate need of supplies and an advance notice to the militia in South Carolina came down from Washington, D.C. that these supplies were going to be sent. The South Carolinians would not hear of it and fired on the fortress sitting at the opening of Charleston's bay, capturing it a day later when the garrison commander began to run out of ammunition.

After Susanna Elliott's untimely death from diphtheria in April, William and Luke managed to keep the ranch running the next several months even though her presence was everywhere around them. The aromas from the kitchen where Lucy fixed fried chicken for them, the smell of the wood burning fireplace, the beauty of the bluebonnets in the pastures, and the murmur of Prairie Creek as it passed through the pasture all contributed to the loneliness that the two men felt at every turn.

Had it not been for Elizabeth, Luke probably would not have been able to handle his mother's passing because they had been so very close when she was alive and the emptiness that prevailed was now filled by Elizabeth's presence.

Their wedding plans for April were put on hold during the period of mourning because Susanna had so much wanted to be a part of it and its planning. She was so enamored of Elizabeth that the thought of someone taking her Luke away was much easier than it would have been if Luke had chosen someone else. Instead, sometime in late summer or early fall would be deemed appropriate for the wedding and plans were being made for a celebration at that time.

Luke and Joshua spent long hours discussing the events that had taken place so far and wondered just what was going to happen to the ranching businesses in central Texas since the cattle drives up north to Kansas and Missouri had been put on hold for the duration of the hostilities that were sure to break out throughout the south.

Joshua said that he could not understand why Negroes were enslaved in the first place and why some were free while others were not. Luke spoke of the need for workers on the plantations and ranches to grow and provide the food necessary to feed the rest of the nation and that without the servitude of the slaves this monumental task could not be done. Besides, it was a legal institution, practiced throughout the United States, was not limited to the south, and many members of Congress had their own slaves as well.

Adamantly, Joshua refused to accept Luke's explanation and swore that someday he was going to do something about it, but had no idea as to what he would actually do. Luke tried to explain to him that his family had always been free and that they came to Texas of their own free will, not because they were the slaves of the Elliott family. That the same thing existed for him and that the love of his family by the Elliotts was genuine and would always continue.

Joshua's temper flared from time to time against Luke because of their differences of opinion and what he conceived as Luke's support of the slavery issue and of secession. Luke kept trying to keep peace between them by refusing to talk about it any more because he felt it was beginning to drive a wedge between them. He wasn't about to let his best friend remain so angry that it would affect a lifelong friendship. He believed that slavery was not the only issue at hand, but that it also included the love of their families and homes, the love of their states, and the fear of the northerners who were trying to change it all by placing their priorities on the people of the south.

"Tomorrow's Saturday. Let's go fishing early in the morning and let the politicians worry about everything else going on in this crazy world of ours" Luke said while trying to change the subject. "I'll swing by your house on the way to the river, okay?"

"That'll be good" Joshua added in a low tone. Luke knew right away that Joshua was up to something, but couldn't figure out just what was on his mind.

Luke awoke early the next morning before sunup and rolled out of bed with high anticipation of catching a lot of fish this morning. He thought of one of the last times he and Joshua had gone to the river when the rattler got a piece of Joshua's hand. "Better keep my eyes wide open this time" Luke thought.

Stopping in the kitchen, Luke found that his father had been up for quite some time and was just sitting at the kitchen table sipping on a cup of rather lukewarm coffee. "Didn't hear you get up" Luke said to William.

"Never went to bed" William said sleepily. "I just can't sleep very well any more because I just keep thinking of your mother all the time."

"I know, Papa. I miss her, too" Luke said lovingly as he put his hand on his father's shoulder. Luke and his father had always been very close and this time of trial caused the bond to grow even stronger.

"Joshua and I are heading to the river this morning. Want to come along?" Luke added.

"Thanks, Luke, but I think I'll head out to the north pasture and visit your mother's grave for a while. I always feel a little better when I'm out there talking to her" William said quietly.

Luke saddled up Golden and tied the lunch bag he had fixed for him and Joshua to the saddle ring as he had done so many times before when they headed to the river to fish. Placing his foot in the stirrup, Luke swung up onto the saddle, took the reins in his hand, and headed across to pick up Joshua.

Approaching the house, Luke noticed that Micah was standing in the doorway with the light from the kitchen streaming around him. "Good morning, Micah" Luke called as he approached the door, "Joshua ready yet?" he asked.

"Come on inside, Luke. I have something to tell you" Micah said with disappointment in his voice.

"What's happened?" Luke asked quizzingly.

"Joshua's gone, Luke" Micah said.

"Gone where? We're going fishing this morning. Has he already gone to the river?" Luke wondered.

"He left last night for Mexico" Micah answered.

"Mexico, why on earth Mexico? We're supposed to go fishing" Luke again asked.

"We had words last night. Awful words that cut deeply into all of us and some of them should have been left unsaid. The quarrel got pretty heated and Joshua left the room slamming his door so hard it shook the house. Lucy and I were terribly upset, and Joshua was determined to get his point across to us, but I'm afraid we will never agree with him on this issue," Micah said in a hushed voice.

"What issue?" Luke asked unbelieving what he was hearing.

"The slavery issue. He wants to go help to free the slaves in whatever way possible and we tried to explain to him that eventually the issue would be settled in the United States without much more to do about it and that his getting so violent wasn't going to help the matter at all. We stressed that he was never a slave and neither were we because there were good people like your family who didn't believe that slavery should have been brought about in the first place. We tried to tell him that Texas' goals were to protect the rights that belonged to the state and that the talk of secession would be a terrible mistake for Texas. I know that slavery is bad and I know that you do, too, but convincing Joshua to let things ride for the time being was more than he wanted to hear," Micah explained. "He left without saying goodbye, but left a note to us saying he figures the only way he can live with himself is to get up north somehow and join the Union army."

For the next half an hour, Micah described the formation of the Underground Railroad in the south and how it was helping slaves escape to the north by providing them with safe havens when they left the plantations and ranches. He described that the plan in Texas was for those escaping slaves to be helped into Mexico where they could remain until it was safe for them to resume their lives back in the states. He told Luke that he knew there were federal troops in Mexico that would help Joshua get to the north, probably by sea from Mexican ports, and into the blue uniform of a Union soldier. Micah lamented that he had no idea if and when Joshua would ever return to the Running E because, he admitted, of the harsh words spoken.

Luke was stunned. His best friend had run out on him all because of his being unable to understand the cause of the south.

Remounting Golden, Luke turned her north towards the Circle Bar W.... and Elizabeth.

Chapter Eleven
The Recruitment

Luke wandered into the living room and looked up at the Kentucky rifle hanging above the front door. "Haven't had that down in a long time. Maybe I'll take it out and fire a few rounds to see if I still have that touch" he thought to himself.

Standing on a dining table chair, Luke carefully lifted the long rifle down from its lofty perch and admired its heft and beauty. "Feels good to have this thing in my hands again" he thought.

Walking out into the front pasture by the road, Luke set up a half dozen gourds he found out there and one very old watermelon that had been left over from the harvest. "That'll make a good target!"

Climbing up in an oak tree to get a better view of the targets, Luke reloaded the rifle. Finding a comfortable branch to support him, he laid the long barrel in the vee of two branches to steady his aim. Sighting in on the first gourd some hundred and fifty yards away, Luke began his methodical approach to firing the rifle, took a deep breath, and gently squeezed the trigger resulting in the pop in the powder pan and the detonation in the barrel. The first gourd was history, splattered into bits and pieces. "Still got that touch" he chuckled to himself.

Sighting in on the second, and then the third and the fourth gourds,

Luke dispatched them in due course finding himself feeling a little proud of his ability to pick off objects at such a distance.

The sound of approaching hoof beats interrupted the next shot aimed at the watermelon and Luke turned to see several Confederate soldiers riding towards him down the road. Luke figured they were here to see his father about selling them some of the longhorn herd out in the north pasture, but the lead horseman called the troops to a halt just under the tree where he was sitting.

"Nice shooting, young man" the sergeant commented.

"Thanks" Luke said. "Want to see me splatter that watermelon way out yonder?"

"Gee, son, that's almost two hundred yards away. Can you hit something with that long rifle that far off?" the sergeant asked.

Readjusting the sights and making sure the rifle barrel was just right in the vee of the branches, Luke sends the watermelon jumping about two feet up in the air and disintegrating as it fell to the ground.

"My goodness, son. That's some shootin'" the sergeant commented while the rest of his troop looked on in amazement. "Very well done" he offered. Changing the subject, he said "we're here to talk to Mr. Elliott about providing our brigade with some beef from his herd. Is he home today?" he asked.

"Yes he is and he told me you all were going to be here sometime. I'll climb down and meet you all at the front door" Luke said as he began his descent from his lofty perch in the oak tree.

William and the sergeant discussed the price of the ten longhorns that were needed and asked Micah to get the ranch hands to cull them out and herd them up to the main gate so that the troops could take over and drive them down the road to the encampment.

When they were finished, the sergeant asked William how old Luke was and he answered he's nineteen with a birthday in December. Rising from his chair and heading to the door the sergeant turned and said he wanted to talk to Luke on the way out.

"Have you ever seen a rifle like this one, Luke?" the sergeant asked as he handed a brand new Whitworth rifle to him. "It's a muzzle loader just like your Kentucky rifle, but the range this thing is capable of firing is a whole lot farther than yours."

"Further than a couple of hundred yards?" Luke asked with a raised eyebrow as if in doubt.

"Try eighteen hundred!" the sergeant boasted.

Luke held the rifle to his shoulder liking the fit and marveling at the light weight of it as compared to his long rifle.

"Would I be able to try a shot with it sometime?" Luke asked.

"How about right now? Trooper" he called to one of his men, "take one of those gourds out in the pasture to about a thousand yards and set it up so he can try his aim with my rifle."

The trooper rode out into the field, picking up a large gourd, and continued on out to the range the sergeant had stated. Dismounting, he placed it on a rock so that it could be seen at that distance and offer Luke a good target.

Luke noticed that the rifle had a telescope sight mounted on the left side of it and commented that he had never seen one with a sight on the side, much less a telescope. He placed the barrel on a fence rail after loading the rifle with its strange six-sided bullet, took careful aim at the gourd barely visible to the naked eye, but suddenly within plain view with the aid of the telescope.

After a seemingly long wait, Luke squeezed the trigger not realizing that the Whitworth packed a wallop with its ferocious kick as the bullet left the barrel headed towards its target.

Having been so close to Luke's right eye, the telescope recoiled with the rifle and smacked him a good one. A couple of the troopers chuckled when Luke realized what had happened to him knowing that it had happened to them when they first tried out the new weapon.

Luke was rather startled at the loss of dignity he had just suffered by the telescope striking him rather unceremoniously, knowing he surely was going to have a bruise there, which would probably look more like a black eye than anything.

"Shoulda warned you about that" the sergeant said, patting Luke on the shoulder, "but look at your target out there."

Luke carefully put the telescope back up to his already smarting eye and saw that the gourd was nowhere to be seen.

"You hit that thing dead center with your first shot. Something that took me almost six months to accomplish and you did it immediately" the sergeant boasted. "We need young men like you to fight for the Confederacy and with your obvious skill at shooting a rifle like that you would make a very fine soldier."

Luke thanked the sergeant, handing the Whitworth back with a grin. "But I'm needed here to help my father run the ranch and we have a huge roundup to get started shortly and I'm going to be really busy with that."

As the troopers rode off down the road, the cattle were herded with them kicking up a large amount of dust as they headed towards the Confederate soldiers' encampment.

Luke had a long talk with William following the visit with the troopers and they both discussed the pros and cons of his fighting for the Confederacy what with the ranch to run. But the most important reason for not going was Elizabeth because he knew he would not be able to handle his being away from her for any length of time. He was torn between the love of Elizabeth and the love of Texas knowing that shortly he was going to have to make a decision that would affect them both.

In the late summer of 1861, battles in the south were at full force and news began to filter to Texas of the progress of the war, which was beginning to spread throughout the south. Some of the reports bore good news of how well the southern forces were doing and at other times of battles that had been lost.

Townsfolk in Salem and Austin were beginning to hear the names of places they had never heard of before, but William recognized the battle sites of Virginia like Bull Run and Manassas. He knew that he would be hearing more of battles getting closer and closer to Texas and the perils they would bring.

Still, more strange named places sent people looking at their maps to see where the armies were fighting. Unheard of until now places like Dry Wood Creek, Lexington, Leesburg, Barbourville, and Santa Rosa Island.

From the very beginning of hostilities, the north blockaded the southern ports with ships spread up and down the eastern seaboard and around to the Gulf of Mexico. The south built smaller ships that were faster than the Yankee warships and could slip through the blockade sometimes without being spotted or captured.

Luke and Elizabeth talked about the war constantly and of the fears that horrible things would result from it. They talked of the battles, of those who would never return to their families, the loss of homes to advancing armies, and of the needs of the Confederacy. They also talked of their marriage and when it was to come about.

****

On a warm late summer afternoon in September at the Salem Methodist Church, Luke stood at the altar beside the Reverend McArthur watching Elizabeth and her father walk down the aisle. Luke could hardly contain himself thinking he had never seen Elizabeth so beautiful and that he was so fortunate to have her become his wife.

Joshua stood next to Luke as his Best Man and Jane Wyatt was Elizabeth's Matron of Honor. William sat proudly in the front row pew. He was wishing that Susanna was sitting there with him and thoughts of their happy wedding of so long ago came flooding back.

The church was filled with friends of both families and the parents of the bride and groom beamed with pride at the new couple standing before them.

Elizabeth was wearing the same wedding dress that her mother had worn when she and Stephen were married and carried a bouquet of Texas wildflowers that grew so abundantly in the hill country.

Luke's mind was twittering as he took Elizabeth's hand and they both approached Reverend McArthur standing before them with his Bible in hand ready to join them as husband and wife. "Hi, cowboy" Elizabeth whispered with a wink of her eye. Luke gulped and whispered "Hi" back to her.

After the ceremony, the ladies of the church had prepared a small reception for them out in the churchyard and served cake, punch, and some small sandwiches that Jane Wyatt had prepared that morning.

During the reception, the sergeant from the brigade rode up to the church and sought out William who was visiting with the guests.

"We are pulling out early in the morning and heading for Galveston to help the troops down there who are having trouble with the Yankee blockade that has closed the port. We can't get much of anything in or out of there and we are in desperate need of supplies" he recounted. "That's why I am here. We need ten more cattle and we need to get them now," he added.

Luke, overhearing the sergeant's urgent plea, told William that he would gather the cattle up and drive them down the road to Salem. "Absolutely not!" William spoke. "You stay here with your bride and guests and Micah and I will take care of getting them down to town."

Later, when all of the guests had departed, Luke and Elizabeth wandered down by the creek that ran by the church yard. "Well, Mrs. Elliott, I guess that's that. What do we do now?" Luke added jokingly.

Elizabeth, taking Luke by the hand, said "Let's go home. Let's go to the Running E where we belong."

Riding back to the ranch in the wagon with the moon just beginning to show itself in the eastern sky, Luke put his arm around Elizabeth and thought to himself "just how long can I keep it from her that I have decided to go fight for Texas and the south?"

Chapter Twelve
Hood's Texas Brigade

Christmas season of 1861 drifted in with a blanket of snow that covered the hill country with its glistening whiteness causing the cedar trees to bow gently towards the ground under the extra burden on their branches. Deer tracks led from tree to tree left there by the hungry bucks in search of food in the branches. An occasional rabbit hopped timidly pausing only long enough to scrape away snow in search of the grass that lay hidden underneath.

Jody, Luke's pet deer now a full grown doe, never strayed far from the barn on the cold nights, but this night was awakened by the rattling of deer antlers not far away. She was beginning to realize that she was being called to another life style that would take her away to join other deer roaming the pastures.

In the fall, shortly after Luke and Elizabeth's wedding, news of the Civil War began to flow into Austin on a daily basis. Reports of battles and long lists of casualties were posted outside the newspaper office on the large community bulletin board as soon as they were received always causing crowds of readers to wonder just how long this awful war was going to last. Oftentimes, a gasp would be heard when the name of a family member or friend was among those listed as lost in a battle in some never before heard of location in the east. Eventually, they all figured, the war would come to Texas.

Distinguishing itself in already heavily fought battles was the newly formed Texas Brigade, under the command of General Louis T. Wigfall, comprised of troops from all over Texas and soon joined by others from Georgia, Arkansas, and South Carolina. The troops that William Elliott had sold the cattle to earlier in the year had, in fact, become a part of the brigade and the invitation to join them still weighed heavily on Luke's mind.

Luke knew that he had to tell Elizabeth soon that he wanted to join the brigade, but decided to wait until after the festivities of Christmas so that his decision wouldn't ruin them for her. He knew also in his heart that Elizabeth would not want him to go and the decision was about to tear him apart with worry.

Christmas Eve services at the Salem Methodist Church began with singing of carols and the traditional pageant when the children acted out the parts of Mary, Joseph, the shepherds, and the Wise Men. The part of the baby Jesus was a small doll that belonged to one of the little girls in the congregation and was carried with the utmost care as if it were a real child.

The light from the church spilled out on the snow covered ground casting an orange glow. Music from the choir and the congregation could be heard throughout the town and thoughts of the war were replaced for the moment with those of good will towards men.

Elizabeth, holding on to Luke's arm as they sang, leaned over to him and whispered "happy birthday, Cowboy!" And after a short pause looked up at him and said "don't you think it's time for you to start thinking about Texas for a change and go ahead and join that brigade you've been wanting to join for several months now?"

Luke was absolutely flabbergasted. He could hardly believe that Elizabeth had actually encouraged him to go off to fight for Texas. After all, he had worried for two or three months just how he was going to break the news to her without upsetting her and here she had almost packed his saddle bags for him to go.

Holding her hand in his calloused hand, he squeezed it to let her know that he was eternally grateful to her for making his decision come so easily.

The new year of 1862 brought news that Abraham Lincoln had officially declared that a state of war now existed and had ordered all federal forces to begin a unified advance deep into the southern states. One of the first of the major cities to fall to the Union army was Nashville right in the middle of Tennessee with expectations that they would continue all the way to the Gulf of Mexico.

It was time for Luke to go and preparations were made for his departure early one February morning. William had assured him that he and Micah could handle the affairs of the ranch and with Elizabeth's help were sure to obtain more contracts with the Confederacy to supply it with a steady flow of beef for the troops. The drovers no longer had to worry about the long drives up to Kansas and Missouri when all they had to do now was herd the cattle into Austin where they were then shipped by rail to wherever they were most needed.

William reached over the door to take the Kentucky rifle down from its perch and remembered how he had left this very ranch so long ago with this same rifle and headed east with Sam Houston towards San Jacinto. He now wanted Luke to carry it with him in an easterly direction again, this time towards the Carolinas and possibly Virginia to use against those who were trying to put Texas in danger again.

Just before sunup, Luke finished loading his saddlebags with the few belongings he felt were necessary to take with him into Austin where he was to begin his participation in the war that seemed to be getting closer to Texas every day. A clean shirt that Elizabeth had smoothed the wrinkles out of the night before and a pair of pants were about all that one side of the bags would hold. The other side was filled with shot for the long rifle, his powder horn, some hardtack and jerky, and the Colt pistol he had won at the county fair. The night before, Elizabeth gave Luke the locket that she had worn for so many years that now had his picture in it alongside the one of her. She placed it around his neck and he promised that he would wear it until he came home again.

William took his gold watch from his watch pocket, wound it carefully, and placed it in Luke's hand. "This was my father's watch as you know. He carried it with him when he was with Andrew Jackson in the battle of New Orleans, I carried it at San Jacinto, and now I want you to carry it wherever the battles take you" he said with a tear in his eye. "It has only one requirement attached to it," he added, "you must bring it back safely upon your return to Texas."

Shaking his father's hand and then Micah's, Luke gave Lucy a big hug and whispered to her to please take care of all of them for him. Nodding her agreement, Lucy patted him on the shoulder and spoke in a soft voice "God be with you, Luke." Looking again at his father, Luke went to him and gave him a final hug promising to return the watch to the Running E as soon as he could.

Walking to the front porch with Elizabeth, Luke took both of her hands in his and stared for a long time into her deep blue eyes once again remembering how many times he had been held in her sway just by doing this. Only this time there were tears in her eyes as she realized this was good bye for a while and that there was the ever present chance she would never be able to look up into his again.

"Don't worry, Elizabeth" Luke calmly said to her. "I'll be back before long and we will have another of our picnics at the creek and forget about what lies before me now." And with that, he held her very close to him, kissing her first on the forehead, then her nose, and then a last kiss good bye.

Holding Elizabeth real close again, Luke promised her that he would be very careful and would return to her one day riding down the very road on which he was about to leave.

Elizabeth stood on the porch long after Luke had disappeared down the road to Salem and Austin and thought that a picnic will be something to look forward to. "I wish I had told him", Elizabeth thought. "I wish I had told him that he is going to be a father in August."

Chapter Thirteen

Marching Orders

The next several months of early 1862 witnessed the fight for the Confederacy take twisted turns from time to time with overwhelming victories and tragic losses for the valiant troops that were now spread in strength from Texas to the Carolinas.

Luke's arrival in Austin in February was on a day that hundreds of young men were already enlisting and being taken by train to Vicksburg, Mississippi, to begin their training to become Confederate soldiers. It was a day of no exception for him. Luke was sworn in by the officer in charge of the new recruits and assigned to the 5th Texas Infantry Regiment, which was to be a part of the Texas Brigade, already a huge segment of the Army of Northern Virginia.

Several dozen young men were literally herded to the train depot down Congress Avenue near the bridge that crossed the Colorado River and placed on board with no particular instructions except that the gruff looking sergeant was in charge and would tell them what to do and what to expect on their two day journey to Vicksburg.

Luke found himself a seat next to a window that was partially open which let in the cold air and would probably need to be closed once the train began to roll because of the smoke from the coal fired engine up ahead. Placing his saddlebag on the ledge overhead he then stowed his long rifle next to him by the window. He had seen these trains from a distance before and always wondered what it would be like to travel to some far off place in search of adventure. Little did he know at the time that he was now embarked on the adventure of a lifetime. One that would remain etched in his mind forever.

As the train pulled out of the Austin depot, the sergeant came into the railroad car and began talking in a loud voice, issuing commands that to some made no sense, but to Luke who was trained to follow instructions were understood completely. The first bit of information the sergeant told the men was that food for them would be served at regular intervals while they were enroute to Vicksburg, but that the sleeping accommodations were to be where they sat which meant there would be two days of sitting on these hard seats contributing to a rather uncomfortable trip.

As the first day began to pass, Luke's thoughts were of Elizabeth and the ranch and how much he already missed being home, but he quickly turned his thoughts towards the anticipated action ahead. He was on his way to fight for Texas and was determined to do his very best for the honor of his family and for the Lone Star State.

One of the first things Luke learned upon the arrival at Vicksburg was that General John Bell Hood had taken command of the Texas Brigade and it was now referred to as Hood's Texas Brigade. This name was destined to be written in history as one of the most honored brigades of the war with a reputation of being extremely fierce fighters who could accomplish any given assignment with amazing results. It also would be known as one which suffered devastating casualties throughout the war.

Vicksburg was a beautiful southern town sitting high on the east bank of the mighty Mississippi River which flowed below on its way to the Gulf of Mexico. Its citizens were very proud people who loved their city and were destined to do all they could to protect it from harm from the Yankee invaders. The presence of the swelling ranks of Confederate soldiers gave them extra courage to face the uncertain future of the South because they knew that the river traffic was a highly sought after asset by both the North and the South as a passageway for supplies to the troops.

For the first couple of weeks that Luke was there the daily routine of close order drill, military tactics, and the installation of military law and order that some of the young men had a hard time accepting. However, the new recruits quickly began to understand the need for this in the military because without it there would be not battlefield discipline and the casualties would be staggering. Men had to learn to obey orders from their superiors without question since their very lives depended upon it.

New gray uniforms of the Confederacy were issued to replace the civilian clothes that were first worn by the new recruits when they arrived and for many, this was the first new set of clothes they had received in years.

Some of the new soldiers had not had any formal training in firing rifles since most of them had come from the cities where the use of rifles was not necessarily a part of their daily routine. Luke was one of the exceptions as he already was an expert shot with the long rifle and proved it over an over again during target practices. Many times he coached the soldiers in proper loading, aiming, and squeezing of the trigger so that they hit the targets instead of wild shots into the air. Luke trained soldier after soldier showing them the proper rifle procedure and became so adept at this training that the sergeant mentioned to the company commander that Luke was a natural leader and should be placed in a position of authority.

After a month of training, word began to filter down through the ranks that the soldiers in the 5th Texas Regiment were about to leave for the long trek to Tennessee where the Union Army was massing its troops for attacks into Mississippi. Luke received word from the sergeant that the company commander, Captain Conway, wanted to see him immediately. Setting the letter he was writing to Elizabeth aside for the moment, he tidied himself up and hurried to the tent where the captain was expecting him. Wondering just what in the world he was being singled out for, Luke ran through his mind every thing that he had done for the last several days and could come up with nothing worthy of being called before the officers for some infraction of the rules.

Stopping at the entrance to the tent, Luke said "Private Elliott reporting as directed, sir." Captain Conway motioned for Luke to come inside the headquarters tent and take a seat which he did rather hesitantly. "The sergeant has noted that you have been helping the new recruits with their rifle practice so much that almost every one of them is now considered an expert rifleman, thanks to you" the captain said proudly. "I see from your records that you have an extensive background in hard work in running a ranch with your family and that you also can splatter a melon at two hundred yards with your long rifle. The Confederacy needs young men like you in positions of leadership and I am now promoting you to sergeant" he added.

Luke gulped and stood up at attention and managed to get a "thank you, sir" out of his mouth. "I'll do my best."

****

The long march northward towards the Tennessee border took several days and word from the scouts that reported back to the brigade indicated that battle with the Yankees was imminent, but just where it was to take place was yet to be determined. All indications were that it would be somewhere near the Tennessee River probably near a small town named Shiloh.

The first few days of April gave Luke little time to prepare his troops for the battle that was about to begin, but his words of advice were mainly to keep their calm and to protect their powder from the dampness of the swampy lands they were about to cross. He remembered when his powder got wet once before back in Texas and his long rifle sputtered and wouldn't fire at all.

At night, the marching troops set up their campsites, built the cookfires, and went about preparing their meals. Luke's experience of helping "Cookie" on the trail drives made him popular with the troops because he seemed to be able to make even the blandest of foods taste like gourmet meals.

Each night, the bugler would blow "Taps" on his bugle at ten o'clock and became the most hated man around when he would blow "Reveille" at four thirty in the morning. The men would dress for the days march, take down their tents, eat a cold breakfast of biscuits swallowed with bitter coffee, and be on the march again by five thirty. The march toward Shiloh was broken only occasionally for a brief rest and for lunch. The rest of the time the march continued northward.

The battle of Shiloh was to cause the most casualties of any battle seen in America before and the tides of battle changed from the North to the South and to the North again time after time. Luke found himself in the thick of the fighting continuously and because of the terrain of the countryside, he discovered that he could climb a tree to get a better shot at the enemy soldiers before him.

Luke positioned himself about ten feet up a tree one morning and waited for the sun to rise so that he could get a better observation point. Clearly with his binoculars he could see Yankee troops away in the distance and cradled his long rifle in a fork of the tree to give it better stability. He spotted a Yankee rifleman climbing a tree about a hundred yards away and took careful aim down the long barrel and began his methodical process of squeezing the trigger. When the smoke cleared from the front of his rifle, Luke saw the rifleman fall backwards and out of the tree. Obviously, his aim was deadly and the crumpled blue uniform at the bottom of the tree proved it conclusively.

Reloading, Luke prepared to fire again at whatever target presented itself when the whine of bullets passing close to him and through the leaves of the tree indicated that the sharpshooters on the other side had spotted where he was and he had better skedaddle in a hurry to another spot. Climbing another tree nearby, Luke positioned his rifle and took aim again and again at the Yankees across the clearing dispatching several with his deadly aim. By noontime, Luke counted seven occasions that his shots had found their marks and the thought of having to shoot enemy shoulders began to weigh heavily on his mind. The thought of killing another person was almost repulsive to him, but realizing that the Yankees were trying to do to him what he was doing to them, he put the thoughts from his mind with the determination that he was going to do all he was capable of doing with his rifle and his keen aim.

Shiloh was a disaster for the South. The original plan was to drive the Yankee forces northward and away from Mississippi, but the overwhelming strength of the Union army counterattacked the Confederates at every turn and caused a very disturbing retreat for them.

With the experience of Shiloh behind them, Luke and Hood's Texas Brigade regrouped, took care of the wounded, buried the dead, and marched on towards Richmond, Virginia, where they were to join forces with the new commander of the Army of Northern Virginia, General Robert E. Lee.

The Battle of Seven Pines and The Seven Days Battles lasted into July of that year with devastating losses for both sides followed by Antietam and Lee's retreat into Virginia in September.

While at Antietam, Luke's marksmanship was legendary with over fifteen Yankee soldiers dropped in their tracks from shots fired from his father's Kentucky long rifle which had done away with a number of Mexican soldiers at the Battle of San Jacinto not thirty years earlier. But the long rifle had its drawbacks in that it took so long to reload and the range was still only about 200 yards. That's when Luke was presented with one of the newer Whitworth rifles with a deadly range of almost one mile, an incredible distance.

The Whitworth rifle fired a very strange .45 caliber bullet that had six sides to it. The barrel of the rifle actually had a twist bored into it which gave the bullet a spin as it left the chamber and out the open end of the barrel. It was a muzzle loader just like the Kentucky rifle, but it had the added advantage that Luke had discovered that day at the ranch when he fired the sergeant's rifle…..a telescope!

Luke liked his long rifle, but he was very proud of the new Whitworth and the advantage it gave him with the telescope. The drawback was that it produced a powerful kick and would often jam the eyepiece of the telescope back into the eye of the shooter producing a rather noticeable black eye. After a while, Luke's troops began to call him "Black Eyed Luke" which, in a way, was a compliment awarded because of his deadly aim.

Luke's precision with the new Whitworth required a strenuous schedule of practice during the lulls of battle. His favorite time with the rifle was to see if he could hit a fence post some 1000 yards away causing it to shatter into hundreds of pieces when struck by the enormous bullet. He knew that if an enemy trooper got in its way during battle that the chance of his survival was virtually nothing. And this worried him. He knew that the Yankees had the faster breech loading Sharps rifle and that their bullets were .52 caliber. Knowing the damage they could do to him kept him busy practicing when time would allow. He also knew that the Yankee snipers were on the lookout for shooters just like he was and if ever captured, whether it be a Yankee or a Rebel sharpshooter, they were considered a hefty prize.

What to do with the Kentucky rifle became a problem for Luke because he couldn't march with two rifles over his shoulders for days on end and he didn't want to just toss it away or give it to some other soldier. Making a deal with the sergeant in charge of the cook wagon, he wrapped it in canvas and strapped it under the wagon securely where it traveled from battle to battle.

Luke was fortunate to receive a letter now and then from Elizabeth, but he knew that letters to her were few and far between because of the battles he had been engaged in for the last several months. It actually was a miracle that any mail got through the lines because armies from each side made it a practice to capture as much as possible not only for the intelligence the mail provided, but also for the low morale it caused when there was no news from home.

It was after the Battle of Fredericksburg that Luke finally received a letter from Elizabeth written in late August that brought him the unexpected news that William Stephen Elliott had been born on August 11th. For the longest time Luke could not believe the good and unexpected news he had just read and stood under a tree gazing up at the stars shining through the branches drinking in the realization of this miracle that had happened back in Texas. Elizabeth had named the baby after its two grandfathers which made them especially proud and she had written that she hoped Luke would approve of this decision. She also added that she was calling him Bill and hoped that Luke would like that as well. Luke, of course, thought to himself that is exactly the choice of names that he would have suggested had he been there when he was born. Oh, how he missed her and Texas and longed for his return there to all of his family once again.

As Luke sat alone in his tent that night he suddenly realized that this was Christmas Eve and his 21st birthday. The most wonderful present he could ever hope to receive was the announcement that he was now a father and the news had come on this very day.

Off in the distance, Christmas carols were being sung by several soldiers and Luke hummed along with them as he began to recall the Christmases he had spent at home.

Prior to turning in for the evening, Luke penciled a letter to Elizabeth telling her how proud he was to be a new father and to wish her a merry Christmas not knowing how long it would take for this letter to find its way all the way back to the ranch in Texas. Probably would be springtime before she gets it, Luke thought before drifting off to a well earned sleep.

Chapter Fourteen
Another Year Passes

It has now been a year since Luke left the ranch to join the Confederate Army in its fight to preserve the South, its traditions, and its livelihood. The war was not going well for the Confederacy and casualties continued to mount after each battle with the Yankee forces. The 5th Texas Regiment had taken its share of losses including a lot of Luke's closest friends which left him in a serious state of sorrow and depression. His attitude was beginning to take on a "kill or be killed" method of fighting the enemy and he found himself taking too many unnecessary risks just to try to eliminate as many of the enemy soldiers that he possibly could.

Understanding Luke's dismay, Captain Conway felt that it was needed for Luke to take a break from the serious fighting and act as a courier of messages among the 1st and the 4th Texas Brigades. For a couple of weeks, Luke rode back and forth between the other commands with maps, plans, and personal messages between the officers which made Luke feel as if he were being punished for being such an excellent sharpshooter with the goal of ending the war single handedly as soon as possible. He understood, though that the new assignment would give him the rest he so desperately needed from the heat of the battles in which he had been continuously involved. Little did he realize that the war would last another two years and that each battle would be more devastating than the last.

Earlier in January 1863, dispatches from General Lee's headquarters filtered down to the Brigade that President Lincoln and the congress in

Washington had passed the Emancipation Proclamation which freed all slaves throughout the southern states. Of course this did not sit well with the Confederacy because it meant the immediate loss of field hands so necessary for the huge plantations and ranches. It would change forever the way of living for so many thousands of land and ranch owners and was sure to create animosity between white and black people for years to come. The freeing of the slaves now meant the South was fighting the North just for a way of life that had existed for over two hundred years.

The Confederates learned that General Ulysses S. Grant had been summoned by President Lincoln to head the Army of the West, the Union Army which would virtually destroy the south in the years remaining in the war.

But the South had plans of its own. General Lee led other Rebel forces in battles in Virginia and fought fiercely at Chancellorsville inflicting heavy casualties on the larger Union forces. His plans were to direct the Confederates on a northerly push into Pennsylvania. It was here that Luke felt the force of a slug from a Yankee sniper who had drawn a bead on him when he was climbing down from a tree where he had been shooting across an open field at enemy soldiers in a trench.

The hot lead creased Luke's upper left arm narrowly missing a hit on the bone, but gouging a wound that hurt like the very dickens. Luke dropped to his knees and hid behind the tree trunk as another bullet whizzed past him and lodged in a tree just behind him. Seeing that his arm was bleeding badly, Luke remembered his training on the ranch and pulled a bandana from his pocket and wrapped it around the opening to stop the blood flow. After a few minutes, he made a dash further back into the woods to the aid station where the medics were already tending to the wounds of other soldiers.

Luke's concern for his own wound vanished when he saw the magnitude of injuries to his fellow soldiers that were in many cases to prove fatal. Bones shattered, flesh wounds bleeding, and cries from the surgical tent where the doctors were operating on those whose injuries would cost the removal of a leg or an arm as a result of their severity. Because of the lack of anesthesia throughout the war, operations were performed with the patient sometimes fully conscious and biting on a piece of leather or occasionally a bullet to help take their minds off of the pain while other medics held him down to keep him from thrashing about. At other times the wounded soldier was probably unconscious or maybe even dead before he could be carried to the operating table.

The severity of soldier's wounds was increased by the oftentimes use of "grape-shot" in the cannons that would fire directly into the advancing lines decimating all who got in the way of the scattering fragments of metal that were stuffed into the barrels before firing. These lethal bits of metal usually were smaller bullets, nails, or scrap that had been cut down to stuff into the barrel and when fired would expand cutting a swath sometimes twenty yards wide. This method of shooting was used extensively by both sides against the long lines of advancing soldiers who would march shoulder to shoulder into the paths of the projectiles. The casualties were always enormous.

After bandaging his own wound with strips of cloth from the aid station, Luke stopped for a moment and took a drink from a nearby water barrel. Gathering his wits about him again, he picked up his Whitfield, reloaded it, and headed back out to the front line to see if he could spot the Yankee who missed him with his shot from his Sharps rifle.

Finding a different tree this time, he shinnied up as quickly as he could and began the search of the trees across the clearing for any telltale signs of gunsmoke from an enemy sniper. Placing his right eye to the telescope, Luke swept the barrel of the rifle slowly back and forth searching each tree or mound for any sign of a barrel or blue uniform when suddenly he spotted a bluecoat straddling a branch high in a big oak tree. Luke could not only see the Yankee sniper's rifle placed in the fork of a branch, but he also could see him leaning back on the tree trunk reaching into his pocket for tobacco to make a cigarette. "Stupid Yankee," Luke thought. "He shouda hid himself better than that behind the trunk instead of resting in front of it. That idiot is gonna sit there and smoke a cigarette and he's making one right now!" Luke grinned. "Doesn't he realize I can see his smoke when he blows it?" Watching the sniper carefully placing the tobacco on the piece of paper, rolling it into the form of a cigarette, running his tongue down the paper to seal it, placing it to his lips, then reaching for a match to light it with, Luke squeezed the last ounce of force on the trigger necessary to send his Whitworth bullet across the field with amazing speed to strike the opposing sniper square in the chest before he could ever get it lit and knocking him clean off the perch, falling some twenty feet into a heap at the bottom of the tree. "One more," Luke thought.

By now, Luke had lost count of those that he had managed to knock out of trees, but he knew it must by now be a staggering sum.

Hood's Texas Brigade followed General Lee into Pennsylvania in June towards a small country town named Gettysburg where the South's continuing history was to be made charging an otherwise never before heard of hill called Cemetery Ridge. It was here at this battle that General Lee finally realized that the battle for the South was becoming more and more hopeless.

The Battle of Gettysburg lasted for three deadly days and it seemed impossible that the South could withstand many more losses of men of such depth that this particular battle would inflict. The North was no exception because their losses were equally as heavy, but because of the size of the reinforcing Union Army its overwhelming forces defeated the Southern forces and pushed them into a retreat back towards Virginia.

By this time, word came that Vicksburg had fallen to General Grant and his army after being held under siege for almost two months. Union forces had surrounded the beautiful city on all sides with massive numbers of troops and lined the Mississippi River with gunboats keeping all means of escaping impossible. Short of starving to death because of the lack of food supplies, the Confederates had no other choice but to surrender the city to General Grant thus dividing the South and its supply lines into two parts. Further losses at Chattanooga in late 1863 drove the terror of war further and further into the South with the Union forces taking their revenge upon the Rebel fighters at almost every battle.

Luke's second year away from home was drawing near. Fortunately, he had received several letters from Elizabeth keeping him informed of Billy's growth, news of how his dad was doing, reports of the ranch, and of her longing to have him return home safely.

She often would ride with William when he was working the pastures to round up the cattle for shipment to Austin and would secretly laugh hoping that some of this beef would find its way to Luke's camp and provide him with a meal sent from home. William loved to have Elizabeth's company because she had helped so much after Susanna's untimely death. Of course, he missed Luke terribly and worried about him constantly hoping that he would return safely after this awful war was over.

Elizabeth wrote often of the shortages of certain things like wheat for bread or material for clothing, but stressed that they were doing all right and provided for themselves whenever possible. The costs of all supplies had risen to prices unheard of before, but accepted as the result of the war and the needs of the troops fighting for them. Elizabeth always talked of the picnic that they were to have upon Luke's return and looked forward to the time when he could take Billy on rides to the north pasture to check the cattle there.

Austin was in a turmoil because of the war, but things remained as normal as could be expected when the threat of Yankee soldiers invading Texas cropped up now and then in the newspapers. The once hoped for early end of the war had faded long ago when the dreams that a victorious South would triumph were crumbling on a daily basis. The posting of casualties outside the newspaper building always drew a large crowd. Whenever Elizabeth went into Austin she, too, would scan the lists hoping not to find Luke's name as a part of them. It was always a relief to walk away from the crowd knowing that her husband was still safe, but hearing the cries and sobs of those who were not so fortunate as she.

Christmas 1863 came and went without much of a celebration at the ranch except for the church services held on Christmas Eve.

Luke's birthday was spent in another tree, watching for movement in any direction that might indicate enemy soldiers approaching.

A new name in early 1864, which would strike fear in the hearts of southerners, was to enter the fray as the new commander of the Union Army of the West when General Grant is named to command all of the armies of the United States. That name was General William T. Sherman whose army would later devastate Atlanta and a good part of Georgia.

1864 battles were numerous, costly in lives, and to the Confederate soldiers, never ending. Places like Cabin Creek, Gimbel's Landing, Fort Wagner, Cox's Plantation, Stony Ridge, and Charleston Harbor were unknown before the war, but would take their places in history as battles where thousands of soldiers both North and South fought with everything they had. For the South, supplies were becoming more and more scarce. There was one battle that gave some little hope to the South, but placed fear in the eyes of Texas when Yankee gunboats made an attempt to sail up the Sabine River separating Texas from Louisiana to capture Fort Griffin upriver.

Fort Griffin, considered by Confederate soldiers to be the last place they wanted to be stationed, was the place for misfits and undesirables to be sent as a discipline measure. Those that were there had little to do, but entertained themselves by target practicing with the fort's cannons by shooting at barrels floating at varying distances apart in the river.

This amusement saved Fort Griffin from falling into Union hands when the riverboats were driven away by well placed shots from the cannons the "bad boys" had mastered so cleverly. A glimmer of hope spread throughout the Confederacy with this little bit of good news of a small victory.

Prior to the campaign at Cold Harbor, Virginia, Hood's Brigade camped for a short while to prepare for the upcoming battle. Troops cleaned their rifles and cannons, washed their clothes in nearby creeks, bathed for the first time in weeks for some men, and wrote letters home.

It was times like this when an army could take a breather from battle that the cooks endeared themselves to the troops by preparing warm food for them at the campsites. It wasn't always like home cooking, but better than hardtack biscuits which were a staple for the soldier on the move. Hardtack was a cracker that was baked at the factories and shipped in crates to the supply depots for further distribution to the troops in the field sometimes months later. The taste of the crackers depended on just how long ago they were made and usually was pretty good. However, when most of the troops received them they were getting very stale and often contained weevils which had made their homes in the crackers. Generally, soldiers were issued a "ration" of these morsels twice a week or so.

Meals at the Confederate campsites usually consisted of salted meat, dried fruit, coffee, sugar, and the hardtack crackers when the supply trains could get them to the troops. One of the favorites for the troops was a mixture of cornmeal, cooking oil, milk, salt, and soda and baked over the open fires. They called them "Johnny Cakes". For troops on the move, a concoction of fried bacon and corn meal could be fixed rapidly and was called "coosh".

Men would gather together sometimes and cook their own meals with whatever food they could get issued to them or that they could pillage while traveling. Again, Luke's experience of cooking on the cattle drives made him a favorite person to have around at meal time because he could make hardtack taste like manna from Heaven with just a little something extra added to the mixture.

Hood's Texas Brigade made its move into Atlanta to defend the stronghold of the deep South. They were joined by regiments and brigades from several other armies and prepared to repel the advances that were to come from the Union Army of the West now under the command of General Sherman.

Atlanta was crucial to the South since it was the major rail center as well as a highly industrial town. It also stood as the symbol of the southern way of life and the citizens were hard pressed to realize that for the most part their beautiful homes and plantations were about to be destroyed by the eventual fall of Atlanta.

Battles waged continuously around Atlanta and names of cities such as Marietta, Peachtree Creek, and Kennesaw Mountain were to be added to those whose fates would be added to infamy. Hood's Brigade retreated further into the city in an attempt to save it, but Sherman's forces inflicted heavy loss of life and the battle was about to come to an end. In its retreat, Hood's forces blew up all the supply dumps it was forced to leave behind to keep them from falling into the hands of the rapidly overtaking Yankees.

Luke and several of his sharpshooters located a house that overlooked the area that the Union forces were expected to make their charge and set up their rifles preparing for the fight. Several of the advancing troops met the shots from Luke's group and went down in the fields not to rise again. All was going well until a sudden blast from a Union cannon tore open half of the wall of the house where they were and a hasty retreat was necessary to save themselves from the deadly fire. As Luke made a dash from the front of the house he noticed a name over the front door and joked to one of his escaping buddies that he hoped Mr. and Mrs. Potter wouldn't mind too terribly much of their making such a mess of their house.

After two months of fighting, Atlantans realized the city was about to fall and set about seeking some terms of surrendering the city to the Union army. The mayor, James Calhoun, upon the encouragement of several citizens who were Northern sympathizers who were called "scalawags" met with Union officers and offered the city to them.

General Sherman then telegraphed President Lincoln that "Atlanta is ours, and fairly won".

Destroying most of the rest of Atlanta, General Sherman then in November 1864 began his massive month long "March to the Sea" and headed his men towards Savannah three hundred miles to the southeast on the coast. Leaving a burned out path over sixty miles wide, Sherman leveled everything in his way as punishment to the South. Capturing Savannah, General Sherman again wired President Lincoln this time offering the city to him as a Christmas present.

What was left then of Hood's Texas Brigade after retreating from Atlanta made their way towards Nashville to help defend that Tennessee stronghold. It was here that these Rebel soldiers were to face a new enemy.... one they never thought they would have to fight. Negro soldiers were now wearing Union blue.

Chapter Fifteen
A Careful Aim

Facing odds of two fresh Union soldiers to every one rag-tag Confederate was too much for General John Bell Hood to withstand after his famous brigade made a heroic attempt to save Nashville from capture, but failed to do so. In December 1864, the tired general resigned his command position and left Tennessee.

He had tried on so many occasions to rally the South to victory and in some battles did exceptionally well, but the better trained, better fed, and better battle seasoned Federal soldiers and their massive resources of manpower were finally suppressing the Confederate Armies into submission.

In early 1865, the Confederate Vice President, Alexander Stephens, met with President Lincoln in Virginia to discuss the terms for peace and hopes were high on both sides that the war which had lasted for four long years might actually be coming to an end. All hopes were dashed when an agreement could not be negotiated and the war would go on for a while longer.

The remnants of Hood's Texas Brigade had dispersed and joined other regiments wherever they could be found. Most of what was left of Luke's old outfit was still under command of Captain Conway and they joined up with Lee's remaining army in preparation for an assault on Petersburg, Maryland. This bloody battle would prove to be the last one that Luke would take his sniper's position in some lonely tree waiting for an unsuspecting Yankee trooper trying to hide in a trench or behind a tree.

General Lee ordered the Army of Northern Virginia to attack Petersburg knowing full well that General Grant was waiting for him there with his huge army. Once again fighting at its fiercest broke out along the battle lines with cannons roaring, rifles firing, and bullets flying in every direction. Casualties were high on both sides, but one on the Confederate side would affect Luke directly with the loss of Captain Conway who fell leading his troops across a clearing and died a heroic death.

Luke, realizing that this may be the last battle he would have to participate in had mixed feelings of jubilation and fear. He was glad that the war was just about over, but terribly sad to realize that the South would never be the same again. Keeping in mind that he still had a job to do, he climbed an oak tree once again and took up his sniper's position with a watchful eye towards the Yankee line.

For some reason, the sound of bullets and the blasts of the cannons seemed to be subsiding. Things were getting quieter as if both sides were waiting to see who would fire the last shots when Luke spotted what appeared to be a blue uniform creeping down a fence line about a thousand yards away. "Ah, ha." Luke thought to himself. "Here's one sneaking down the fence line and I've got him in my sights."

Slowly, the figure crept from one fence post to another trying to remain undetected, but Luke followed him with his telescope to his eye just waiting for him to get a little closer. "Just a little bit closer. Just a little bit more. Come on Yankee, just a little more," Luke thought as he placed his finger on the Whitworth trigger.

"I can almost make out his face, but he keeps it hidden behind the grass" Luke thought. "I'll give him another few seconds and I'll then introduce him to my Whitworth."

Carefully, carefully Luke trailed the soldier with his telescope as he dodged from fence post to fence post actually believing that he was not being observed by one of the finest sharpshooters the Confederates had.

The time was now. He must make his shot or possibly miss if something should startle the soldier at the last second and he would hate to miss such a perfect target as this.

"Now," Luke thought. Cocking the hammer he placed his right forefinger on the trigger again and began his firing routine that he had been doing since he was a much younger man. "Take a deep breath. Hold it. Aim the rifle perfectly. Take up the fraction of slack….and squeeze," he thought almost out loud. Luke could see the enemy perfectly through his telescope as the hammer ignited the powder in the pan sending the bullet flying across the field towards its target.

Luke continued to watch for a split second through the telescope to see the bullet hit its target and when the smoke cleared from in front of the barrel he saw the Yankee soldier turn abruptly towards him, grasping the side of his head in disbelief, and begin to fall.

To Luke's utter horror he recognized the face in the telescope.

It was Joshua!

Chapter Sixteen

The Promotion

Luke froze in a moment of horror when he realized that the figure in the blue uniform that had been very carefully dodging from fence post to fence post was his dearest friend whom he had not seen in over three years. His mind harkened back to when the two of them chased the fox under the tree, the hornets' nest that gave them a stinging lesson, the lazy days fishing at the river, and the times of just being the best of friends. And he remembered when he learned that Joshua had left the night before to go join the Union forces and the sorrow he had when he realized he may never see him again.

But see him he did.....in the telescope of his Whitworth rifle when the bullet struck him.

Recovering his senses in a quick moment, Luke was determined to get to Joshua somehow. Just how he was to do this would take every ounce of courage that he had left in his tired body, but whatever the choice it would have to be quick and daring. He then realized that a lot of the shooting had paused as if something had called for stillness to reign over the area for a few brief moments.

Dropping down from the tree, Luke propped his rifle against the trunk and fell to the ground to survey just what lay between him and Joshua still crumpled against the fence only a few yards away. Unfolding a bandage from his knapsack, he began crawling through the grass foot by foot fully expecting a shower of bullets to come raining down on him, but so far no one had seen him. An occasional shot would fly over him, but it was not directed at him this time.

Luke crawled towards Joshua who hadn't moved since he was hit. Finally at the fence, he made his way to Joshua and cradled him in his arms as he rocked back and forth. With tears streaming down his face, Luke wiped the blood that was trickling down the side of Joshua's head and dropping on the grass below. "He's alive!" Luke almost shouted out loud. "Joshua….Joshua….can you hear me?" Luke asked. But there was no answer from him. Then taking the bandage he still had in his hand he began to wrap it very carefully around Joshua's head to stop the bleeding when he realized that Joshua was now breathing evenly.

The bullet had just creased Joshua's side of his head causing an ugly tear and knocking him unconscious, but otherwise not a fatal wound.

And there they sat just for a few moments. A Yankee Bluecoat in the arms of a Confederate sharpshooter…..perhaps the best in the whole Southern army…..who had missed an easy target.

"Don't you move a muscle" came a deep stern voice from behind Luke sending chills up his neck. "I mean it, Reb, don't you dare move."

Luke continued to hold Joshua in his arms, but turned his eyes towards the biggest barrel of a gun he had ever seen being held just a few inches from his head. "This is Joshua" Luke said. "He is my closest friend and I've hurt him."

Looking up at the Yankee soldier holding the menacing rifle, Luke realized that it was a Negro sergeant, the first one he had seen in battle.

The sergeant looked down at Luke for a long time and almost smiled. Luke thinking his moment had come to be the recipient of a bullet raised his tear stained face towards the face of the soldier. "You must be Luke" came the strange words from the sergeant. "Joshua has spoken of you often." Dropping to his knee and propping his rifle on the fence, the sergeant took a look at Joshua and muttered "told you to keep your fool head down!"

"He'll live," the sergeant said to Luke, "but only because you came across that field to take care of him. That was a mark of true bravery and of a true friend…..or of a complete idiot…..I'm not sure which. Now…. skedaddle back across that field and get back to your outfit. This war's about over and I don't want to see any more killin'. I'll take Joshua to the medics."

Luke helped lift Joshua onto the shoulders of the Yankee sergeant and turned to leave, but hesitated. "Thank you sergeant for helping me….and for my life….God go with you my friend." Luke saluted the sergeant and began a quick retreat back to his side of the clearing.

Stopping long enough to pick up his rifle, Luke headed back to the campsite when he was approached by one of the troops carrying a message for him to report to headquarters immediately. Not at all sure of just what the summons was for, he stopped at the water barrel for a short drink of water and washed his dirty face with what was left in the ladle.

Major Alexander beckoned Luke into the tent and stood to tell him that Captain Conway had been killed which left no other officer to take charge of the remainder of the brigade. "I am now placing you in charge and promoting you…..Captain Elliott!"

Battlefield promotions were very common during wars and many times enlisted personnel were called upon to step up and fill the shoes of officers who may have been killed or wounded unable to continue in their present position. Luke was one of those personnel who had constantly shown leadership under fire and was now being called upon to continue that leadership as an officer in the Confederate Army.

Luke's knees almost buckled when he realized the awesome responsibility that had just been handed him. He knew the war was just about over and that there probably would not be much left for him to command, but still the thought that he was now directly responsible for the lives of his men left him wondering if he were really capable of carrying out such a promotion.

Captain Elliott and Major Alexander spent the next hour or so reviewing the plans for the coming movement which was to take them south to Virginia again and to Appomattox Court House, a small farming town nestled among the green hills.

They were not to learn until the next day that Richmond had fallen which spelled the beginning of the end for the South.

Marching towards Appomattox Court House, a courier from General Lee's staff rode up to Major Alexander with a message that an officer was to accompany him back to General Lee. "You're the only other one," the major said, "report to the general as ordered….but be careful along the way!"

Spurring his horse to a full gallop, Luke headed directly to the back side of the trees where General Lee's headquarters were located. The sound of an occasional cannon blast in the distance interrupted an otherwise strange silence that had fallen over the entire area for the last hour or so. Reining to a stop at the General's compound, a young private saluted and took the reins to Luke's horse and tied it to the hitching post nearby. "Good afternoon, Captain," the private said. Luke, not yet accustomed to being called by that name almost didn't acknowledge the younger man, but returned the salute smartly as he passed towards the headquarters.

"I'm Captain Elliott from the Texas Brigade and I have been directed to report to General Lee for special orders," Luke said to the officer sitting at the entrance to the command tent. "Right this way, Captain," the officer said directing Luke towards another tent where several other Confederate officers were already gathered listening to a stately gray bearded man whose shoulders the entire South had rested upon. For the first time, Luke had actually seen General Robert E. Lee and now he was in his very headquarters awaiting some special orders from the general that he had no idea what would be.

General Lee approached Luke and looked squarely at him saying "son, I need a special person to deliver a very important message to General Grant that the very outcome of the war will depend on what he has to say. You will travel to his headquarters under a flag of truce, alone, and present this packet to him personally, wait for his reply, and report to me immediately when you receive it. I have been told that you are an experienced soldier, an expert horseman, a deadly shot with your rifle, and totally dependable for an important mission for the South. I will await your return and report. Good luck, son, you carry a heavy load for me."

Saluting the general, Luke assured him that he would return as quickly as he could with the answer he was waiting for. Taking the packet and placing it in his saddlebag, Luke mounted his horse and prepared to leave when another officer approached him with a white flag made from a piece of tablecloth tied to the top of a tent pole which would signify he was traveling under the protection of truce and would not be fired upon by the enemy…..provided they were honorable and would acknowledge such a signal. Luke asked the officer just what was in the packet that was so important not knowing if the officer would actually answer such a classified question, but was told that General Lee was asking General Grant what terms of surrender he would accept. The officer felt that Luke at least ought to know what he was carrying and the critical importance of the letter.

Approaching the edge of the woods and the safety of the trees, Luke proceeded down the road to the clearing and began to cross the open field towards the Yankee lines just a few hundred yards away. As he rode, Luke looked about him wondering just what reception he would receive as he crossed over to the Yankee line and approached their headquarters. He had heard that they smelled awful, hardly ever bathed, and wore sloppy uniforms all the time.

Heading towards the campsite where General Grant probably would be, Yankee soldiers stopped in their tracks amazed at what they were seeing and could hardly believe their eyes. They had heard that the Rebs never bathed, smelled bad, and wore sloppy uniforms. Here was a Confederate officer astride his horse, neatly dressed, presenting an impressive figure with his six foot three frame, and carrying a flag of truce obviously with something important on his mind. Luke had not been this close to the enemy during the whole war and was astonished to see that they were so many and so well fed because he could smell the delicious aroma of their cook fires and of the delicious meals they probably would be having. Far better than hardtack, he thought.

Luke stopped in front of a group of gathering soldiers and informed the officer that he was under a flag of truce, sent by General Lee with a special packet for General Grant. The officers saluted one another and the Union officer invited Luke to step down from his horse and come with him to the General's tent. "I'm Captain Hall, General Grant's aide," he said. Luke introduced himself and thanked the captain for his courtesies.

Announcing to General Grant that a Confederate officer had arrived under a flag of truce, the officer informed him that he was just outside waiting to present him with a packet from General Lee. "Show him in, Captain. By all means, show him in" Grant shouted.

Luke entered the general's tent, saluted, and said "I am Captain Elliott and I have a personal message to you from General Lee and my orders are to wait for your reply, sir."

Grant, dressed in a blue officers' coat dirty from having been on the move all day, wearing a black hat, was puffing constantly on a cigar when he returned Luke's salute. Taking the packet, Grant unfolded it and sat down to read what Lee had written to him and then read it over again. Calling his aide, General Grant directed him to have two of his generals join him for a meeting.

Captain Hall invited Luke to come outside with him and have something to eat and drink while the generals met and discussed Lee's message. Luke took an immediate liking to his host because he was polite, about his own age, and not at all what he had been led to believe of what Yankee soldiers were. They discussed their families, each telling one another about their earlier years, their wives, and the longing to go home to see them. Captain Hall told Luke that he was a graduate of the United States Military Academy at West Point and had been on active duty for eight years. Luke was very impressed, thinking he not only is a very nice guy, but he's well educated as well.

General Grant burst through the flap at his tent startling the two officers who were sitting casually at a small table having their food. Standing up rapidly in his presence, Luke almost spilled the coffee he had been drinking, but managed to place it gently on the table when the general handed him a packet.

"This is the answer to General Lee's question, Captain. Take it to him quickly with my compliments as one officer to another. My aide will escort you safely through the lines," Grant said.

"Thank you, General. I will be on my way," Luke responded while saluting.

Thanking Captain Hall for his courtesies, Luke waved goodbye to him and wished him well as he turned and headed back into his own Confederate lines and General Lee's headquarters.

Luke had figured correctly in his mind what the special meeting with General Grant was about in that it was leading up to the final step to end the war with the North by surrendering the remaining forces of the South by General Lee to General Grant.

Grant's reply was handed to Lee in person with the explanation that he had spoken directly with the Union commander as he had been ordered earlier.

Placing his hand on Luke's shoulder, General Lee spoke in a quiet voice "well done, Captain. You have just participated in history….a story you can tell your son when you return home."

Saluting the general, Luke walked from his tent with those words ringing in his ears. "Return home……return home," he thought. "Could this be the beginning of the end and maybe I'll be going home soon?"

Walking his horse past the cook wagon, the sergeant offered Luke a cup of coffee and the two of them talked for a while of things in general.

Both noticed as they were sharing these moments that an unusual quiet had fallen over the countryside. A quiet that they had not heard for so many years.

Luke asked the sergeant if his long rifle was still fastened to the bottom of the cook wagon after all this time and he assured Luke that it still was safely there. Now that he was an officer, Luke carried his Colt pistol and the Whitworth rifle was usually in the way. Climbing under the wagon, Luke removed the long canvas bag that had protected the Kentucky rifle and placed his Whitworth in there with it. Making sure the bag was secure once again, Luke commented to the sergeant "probably won't need that for a while!"

Sitting down under a tree for a needed rest, Luke began to recall the earlier events during the last battle at Petersburg and wondered just what had finally happened to Joshua and if he was recovering satisfactorily from the wound he had inflicted upon him.

"I wonder if I will ever see him again?" Luke thought to himself in moment of sadness.

Chapter Seventeen
The Quiet

General Robert E. Lee rode with Colonel Charles Marshall to the three story home of the Wilmer McClean family and stepped down from his white horse, Traveller. Climbing the stairs to the long front porch at the second level, he was met by Mr. McClean and was escorted to the parlor of his home.

Wilmer McClean and his family had lived in Manassas, Virginia, on their farm for several years prior to the outbreak of the Civil War. When the war actually began in what was to be called the First Battle of Bull Run, it was when the Union Army fired at McClean's home, which had been the headquarters of General P.G.T Beauregard of the Confederate Army.

McClean, who had been a Major in the Virginia militia much earlier, decided to move his family to a safer haven in Appomattox Court House, Virginia, deep in the heart of the state to continue his occupation as a sugar broker. The Confederate Army was his biggest client.

Little did he realize that the Civil War that had lasted these past four years which began in his front pasture would actually now end in his parlor!

Lee's thoughts as he entered the now empty parlor, were of the South and of the four long years that had led up to this moment of history that had changed the face of the nation, its people, and its way of life that had so long endured. He was not exactly sure of the reception that he was to receive from those Union officers who would arrive shortly to the parlor to the left of the front door, but he held his six foot frame erect, smoothed his immaculate gray uniform, removed his gloves, and entered.

For almost two hours after his arrival, General Robert E. Lee and General Ulysses S. Grant sat across the room from one another at two different tables and spoke of many things that they had shared in the past because they had been stationed at the same army post together once before. Lee was several years older than Grant, but now they sat together as equals and the commanders of two different armies about to settle the final terms of surrender that the North was offering to the South.

General Grant, as gruff as he usually was, was the absolute gentleman on this day to his great adversary. Rather than the historical precedents of past wars where prisoners were taken and the leaders punished, Grant spoke for the North and offered the Southern soldiers safe passage to their homes rather than to jail cells. All of the officers were to be allowed to keep their sidearms, but the rifles and all military equipment were to be stacked and left behind. The officers could keep their horses and enlisted men could keep their mules and horses if they still had them in their possession. Confederate soldiers would then be paroled by signing a promise that they would never again take up arms against the United States. They would be fed, given enough money to travel, and sent home.

The surrender conditions were most lenient and General Lee accepted them for the South.

Lee mounted Traveller again and saluted General Grant who raised his hat in tribute to his former enemy who was now almost like an old friend. Turning his horse towards the road, the Union troops which had gathered by the hundreds near the McClean home began to cheer that the war was over, but Grant spoke in his loud voice that this demonstration would stop immediately. Instead of jeering, the troops removed their hats in tribute to Lee as he rode past them. Holding his head high, Lee acknowledged these tributes for what they were, but his heart was heavy with the knowledge the South must now begin a long road to recovery and reconstruction.

****

Word was sent to all the armies throughout the south that surrender had been in effect since April 9, 1865, but since the only means of communication was by courier or telegraph, if it was still in operation, it sometimes took many days for everyone to learn that hostilities had ended.

The final battle of the Civil War took place at Palmetto Ranch near the southern Texas city of Brownsville on the Mexican border over four weeks after the surrender at Appomattox.

****

Several days later, gathering his men together Luke passed out the paroles and the mustering out pay they had coming. His final words to them were to be careful on their long treks home and wished for them good fortune in the years to come.

It was a tearful departure for many of the men, but for others a tremendous relief that finally they were heading back to their families that some of them had not seen for over three years.

Hood's Texas Brigade had made history for itself during the war years and had fought gallantly in so many battles that most were hard to recollect by those who had participated in them. Over five thousand Texas volunteers had patriotically joined the Brigade in 1861, but by wars' end only 617 had survived.

As the last of the departing soldiers headed down the different roads towards home, Luke mounted his horse and began to realize just how far he was from Texas, Elizabeth, and the son he had never seen.

Stopping by the abandoned cook wagon, Luke looked around to see if there were any supplies or food that he could gather for his saddlebags. A little coffee, some sugar, an unopened tin of cornmeal, and some rather stale hardtack were about all there was, but Luke was grateful he could find that much. He knew he was going to have to forage for food all the way home if he couldn't find a farmhouse or town where someone would feed him.

"Papa's rifle," Luke suddenly remembered as he knelt down to look under the wagon. There was the canvas bag still firmly tied where he had placed it after Petersburg. "I'll leave the Whitworth here because that's what the orders were, but I'm not leaving Papa's rifle here to rust away," he mumbled to himself.

Pulling the Kentucky rifle from under the cook wagon and removing the canvas wrapping, he leaned it against the wheel of the wagon. Luke held the Whitworth rifle for one last time and admired it for its beauty and thought how lucky he was that a Union soldier had not drawn a bead on him from some distant hiding place like he had done so many times to them. He counted twenty-seven notches on the stock of the rifle and added that figure to the thirteen he had carved on the Kentucky rifle. "Forty", he thought. Forty men who would not be returning to their families ever again because each notch represented a Union soldier that he had seen in his sights before pulling the trigger sending a lead bullet to its mark.

Luke felt saddened for these soldiers who had died for the Union, but thankful that he had received only a flesh wound to his left arm earlier from a soldier whose aim was not as deadly as his. "War is a horrible thing and I hope that I never have to witness it again." Luke thought to himself.

The afternoon sun was rising high over his right shoulder as Luke turned his horse towards Texas. "Let's see…..I'm in Virginia. That means North Carolina, Georgia, Alabama, Mississippi, and Louisiana, before I get to Texas and home. Guess I'd better be on my way," Luke mused.

Breaking out in a nondescript song that was on his mind, Luke suddenly began to sing at the top of his voice.

He was going home!

Chapter Eighteen
Homeward to Texas

Spring had been in full bloom in Virginia for well over a month now. The air was fragrant with the smell of the flowers and of fields of green grass almost as far as the eye could see. Birds were nesting in the tall pines and their songs were echoing across the meadows. The late June sun was warm, but not too hot on Luke's shoulders as he made his way southward towards North Carolina passing through small cities and towns just beginning to come alive again after so long a war that had kept them living in constant fear of battles raging nearby.

Luke was averaging twenty miles each day and by his calculations he should be home sometime in the fall or early winter if all went well during his journey. Riding horseback was second nature to him and the long hours in the saddle were no more tiring than those trailing the herds of cattle on the long drives to Kansas he experienced years ago.

The road sign said Greensboro, North Carolina, ahead fifteen miles. Luke reckoned he could be there before nightfall and would camp somewhere that he could take a bath in a stream and cook some of the beans he had with him in his knapsack. The road to Greensboro looked friendly enough and Luke followed it all the way to the outskirts of town dozing occasionally as the miles quickly passed.

The next morning, Luke saddled up again, broke camp, and entered the town along about sunrise. The local townspeople were just beginning to stir about the streets and the smell of bacon cooking was almost more than he could stand. He always loved bacon as a young boy and sometimes managed to eat at least six or seven pieces at breakfast.

Noticing that the hotel offered breakfast and coffee for twenty five cents, Luke figured he would splurge and treat himself to something decent to eat for the first time since he left Virginia. Wrapping the bridle around the hitching post, Luke entered the café and took a seat at a table near the kitchen door where the aromas of country cooking drifted about.

A young woman brought Luke his long awaited breakfast of eggs, bread, bacon, grits, and lots of coffee which were downed leisurely and deliciously with Luke savoring every bite. An older man struck up a conversation with Luke and began asking him about his experiences in the war since he recognized the captain's uniform that Luke still wore. Luke explained to the gentleman that he had been with General Hood since 1861 and had left Appomattox Court House when hostilities ceased, but was now heading back home to Texas and his ranch.

Luke's experience in Greensboro with the inquisitive gentleman was similar to many he encountered along the way to Texas with persons wanting to know as much as Luke was willing to take the time to tell them. On several occasions, he was invited to their homes and offered dinner and a bed for the night instead of having to sleep in the open on the hard ground.

By late July, Luke had reached the Georgia border and followed the road leading to Atlanta remembering when he was here last during the battle and of the narrow escape from the Potter family home when the artillery shell blew out the wall where they had been only moments before. It was in Atlanta where he first encountered a Carpetbagger.

Already, the federal government had begun to send its representatives into the south to begin reconstruction procedures. Arriving with their suitcases made of heavy carpet....thus "carpetbags", these individuals were often former Union soldiers who had large amounts of mustering out pay in their bank accounts and were intent on furthering their own fortunes by exploiting the southerners who were trying to build their lives and homes again, but oftentimes couldn't afford to pay the heavy taxes being levied on them by the federal government. The Carpetbaggers would then pay the taxes and buy the lands for pennies on the dollar. Lands that the former owners could no longer afford to operate. They were a hated bunch, increasing in numbers almost every day, and spread throughout the south over the next several years.

Atlanta was still pretty much a burned out city, but signs of recovery were beginning to be observed by Luke as he passed through. Some shops were reopening in the damaged buildings and what little local produce that was available was now being offered in some of the stores at an enormous price.

Traveling westward from Atlanta, Luke traveled through Marietta and Kennesaw Mountain heading towards Alabama in August. It was here that Union soldiers surprised Luke one evening and ordered him to stop and dismount.

Luke followed the orders of the soldiers and did what they demanded, but upon producing his parole which guaranteed him safe passage home, the soldiers became more cordial realizing he was an officer and invited him to rest a spell.

Noticing that the soldiers were having a hard time getting a fire going to prepare their evening meal, Luke offered to do it for them saying that he would be willing to cook their dinner for them since he had done it so many times on the cattle trails. The only thing Luke asked in return was to join them for dinner which they willingly accepted.

They all spent a rather enjoyable evening recalling stories of their lives before the war and of what all they did during the war. The soldiers were very impressed with his battle record and commented that they were glad that he hadn't targeted them in his telescope.

Since it was already getting dark, the soldiers offered a spare tent for Luke to spend the night in rather than try to head out to make camp somewhere down the road. As he lay in the tent, Luke chuckled to himself thinking that this was a real turn of events. Here he was, a former Confederate officer, bedding down in a Yankee tent with armed soldiers nearby who had fed him dinner and were looking forward to his cooking breakfast for them in the morning. What a tale this would make he thought as he drifted off to sleep.

Luke was on his way again in the morning and the soldiers had given him lots of provisions that he surely could use on the way home. He was curious why they had not questioned him about the Kentucky rifle he had stretched across the saddle, but figured that since they knew he was an officer that he must have been given the okay earlier to keep it after the surrender. "What they don't know won't hurt them, I guess," he thought as he rode on down the road.

September was almost upon him and he was just outside Birmingham, Alabama, when rains came for days on end slowing Luke's progress to almost a standstill. He had hoped to be in Mississippi by this time, but the muddy roads and swollen creeks caused him to delay day after day in some abandoned barn or partially burned out house. Luke thought that he hadn't seen this much rain since the time the Colorado River rose out of its banks and flooded a good part of Austin. Now he was stuck in Alabama with a long way still to go before he would be home again.

When the rains let up and the water began to recede from the banks, Luke once again was astride his horse heading for the Mississippi border. Turning in a more southerly direction, Luke traveled the next several days riding through the tall pines of Alabama, passing Tuscaloosa, finally crossing the Tombigbee River just before entering Mississippi along about Meridian.

It had been over three years since he was in this state under different circumstances. That was back when he had just left Vicksburg and went north to the Tennessee border near Memphis during the early stages of the war. It was also a time when the South had visions of winning many battles and emerging victorious after the war. But the South was in shambles now because of the war and would be in a state of recovery for so many years to come. Wounds both physical and mental would require a very long time to heal and perhaps for some never would.

In Jackson, Mississippi, Luke decided to rest for a few days before continuing on towards Texas. He had been riding now for three months and was only about halfway home, but he was beginning to tire somewhat and decided rather than chance getting hurt from some stupid accident while not paying attention that he would just rest and sleep for a while. He still had a bit of money left in his pocket and had done fairly well keeping his provisions stocked with whatever food he could find along the way. This time in Jackson, he was going to find a barber to trim his hair and give him a shave after taking a hot bath at one of the local bathhouses.

Pitching his small tent on the banks of the Pearl River, Luke cut a branch from a small tree and fashioned a fishing pole out of it. Attaching a piece of corn to a bent straight pin used as a hook, he tied a ball from a cottonwood tree as a bobber and set about to catch him some fish for dinner. Propping himself up beside the trunk of a weeping willow tree whose branches dipped almost into the flowing water before him, Luke settled back to await the first nibble on the bait.

This reminded him of the hours that he and Joshua had spent fishing in the creek at the ranch just lolling about without a care in the world. Drifting off into a light sleep, Luke was awakened by the tug on his line of a catfish as it took the bait dangling just below the surface of the water. First one, then three more fish were added to the catch, which would provide one of the best trail cooked meals Luke had eaten in years.

Cleaning the fish one by one, Luke spread them out on the hot rocks next to the fire before he skewered them with a willow branch to hang them over the flames to cook. Taking some of the cornmeal, he added a small amount of bacon fat that he had been carefully carrying for a couple of days and stirred them together to make several corn cakes which he cooked on the hot rocks.

Nighttime fell that September evening and Luke crawled into his tent falling fast asleep in just a matter of moments after such a good dinner he had fixed for himself. His last thoughts were of Elizabeth and Bill and he smiled knowing that soon he would be home with them.

Continuing on his way several days later, Luke felt refreshed to the point he thought he could make it to Texas before fall set in. The rest had done him good and the dinners he had cooked even better. He had managed to shoot a small deer on one of his hunting forages while there at the river and he had eaten venison steaks several times. The rest of the meat he set out to dry so that he could pack it away for dinners later on down the road home.

Vicksburg was just over the next hill. It had taken the townspeople many months to recover after Grant had laid siege to the city back in '62 and almost starved them out, but from the looks of things as he rode down the streets things were returning to normal.

This was where Elizabeth used to live, Luke remembered, and set about asking some of the local merchants if they had ever known the Wyatts and where they might have lived when they owned their farm here before moving to Texas. An older woman overhearing Luke asking the mercantile store owner about them, offered that she had known the family when they first came to Vicksburg and had remembered Elizabeth as a beautiful child with long black hair and captivating blue eyes. Luke told them who he was and that Elizabeth was now his wife in Texas.

Giving Luke directions to the old farm house, Luke thanked the lady and headed down the small country road arriving about thirty minutes later. Luke was surprised to see that the house was still standing and now occupied by another family whom he learned were the ones who actually bought the farm from the Wyatts when they left to become ranchers in Texas.

Spending a couple of hours visiting with the family, Luke made his departure and began his westward trek towards the Mississippi River that he knew he had to cross at the ferry. Before he left the farm, Luke gathered up several flowers and pressed them in the Bible that he had carried with him when he went off to war. He wanted to give them to Elizabeth as a reminder of her childhood days here in Vicksburg.

The river loomed ahead, but the ferry had been out of working order for several days and its return to service was questionable. Luke spent the next day and a half trying to find someone who would take him and his horse across the river on their barge and not charge him anything for the passage. A group of Union cavalrymen were heading west to Oklahoma and offered Luke a ride aboard the barge the army had hired to carry supplies back and forth across the river during the absence of the regular ferry.

The wind blew spray from the river across the bow of the ferry as it made its way to the mile distant shore. Right here at this very spot in the river is where the Union gunboats kept the city of Vicksburg at bay. How things have changed. Once again he chuckled at the thought that here he was, a former Confederate officer, out on a boat ride with Union soldiers!

Luke felt a cooler breeze waft across his face. The first sign of fall, he thought. The weather will start getting cooler now that September was almost over and he still had Louisiana and half of Texas to cross before making it to the Running E. But, once again, the rains slowed him down to only a handful of miles each day and those were spent searching for a dry, warm place to camp.

Deciding to turn further southward in Louisiana to avoid the marshes he was encountering, Luke headed towards Natchitoches, a small town alongside the Red River. Even though only a hundred miles from where he was, it took Luke more than a week to plod through the mud and rain and his food supplies were running thin. "Besides," he thought to himself, "if I don't get out of this foul weather soon I'm gonna catch pea-new-monia."

Arriving there late one evening when the rain seemed to be coming down harder and harder, Luke decided to ask the livery stable owner if he could camp out in the barn for a day or two until the rain ended. Finding the owner extremely pleased that Luke would ask to let him stay in the tack room where all the bridles and saddles were stored. There was a cot in the warm and dry room, which Luke welcomed with anticipation of a good nights sleep for a change. Before he turned in, Luke decided to head over to the hotel café for another splurge of his dwindling cash on a good hot meal.

The waitress slapped him on the shoulder as he entered which startled Luke somewhat. "Welcome to the Back Street Café, Captain," she spoke.

"Looks like you've come a long way and needed a place to come in out of the rain, right?"

Luke smiled answering "yes ma'am. I've come from Virginia on my way home to Texas," remembering the questions he received at each place along the way when he ventured into a café or hotel. People were genuinely glad to welcome him and always tried to make him feel comfortable. A lot of times they would add an extra chop or steak for his dinner just to show their appreciation for his service to the South.

Tonight's dinner was no exception. Piled high on his plate were mounds of mashed potatoes and gravy, corn on the cob, green beans that he hadn't tasted the likes of in years, and two huge country fried steaks smothered in onions. As he finished the last bite, the waitress brought him more coffee and a piece of pecan pie to top off a wonderful dinner.

Seeing that the waitress had a tear in her eye, Luke asked her if she had lived here in Natchitoches long, just to start a conversation. Standing by the table she answered that her family had been in this town for two generations, but since her husband had died three years ago she was thinking of moving on to another location. "But," she added, "I'll probably just stay here since I just added my son to the cemetery next to his father and I really want to stay near them….." she said as her voice began to fade. "He was lost in the Battle of Antietam back in '62. Have you ever heard of that place?"

Inviting her to sit at his table, Luke answered "yes ma'am. I was there too."

For a long time, Luke listened to the woman letting her tell in great detail all about her son and how proud she was of him. She listened to him as well as he related to her as much about Antietam as he could remember believing that it would help her recover from her grief knowing about the battle.

As Luke stood to leave the café, he pulled his money from his pocket to pay for his dinner when the waitress placed her hand over his and refused payment. "I'd like to think that someone took care of my son with a warm meal sometime and it would mean a lot to me if you would let me take care of you this evening," she said giving him a hug and a kiss on his cheek.

The rain had let up during the night and Luke packed his belongings into his saddlebags as he prepared to place the saddle on his horse. "Here, let me do that for you Captain," as the stable owner took it from Luke's hands. "Seems that a lot of folks around here wanted to thank you for your service to the South and they packed some supplies for you to take with you to Texas," he added.

Luke was overwhelmed with the generosity of the townspeople and their gift to him, but could hardly believe that most of them lined the street leading out of town to wave good bye to him as he passed by.

"Another seventy five miles to the border," Luke thought. "I should make it there in three days or so if the weather continues to hold and then I'll be in Texas once again."

By now, October had ended and the cold winds of November were about to set upon the weary traveler who had been in the saddle since Appomattox and early June. Five months he had ridden through six states and he still had almost four hundred miles to go before he would be home. Luke had been worried that Elizabeth would be concerned as to where he actually was and tried to send her a letter in Atlanta and a telegram from Vicksburg, but had no assurances that she ever received the news of how he was coming as fast as he could. Of course, he hadn't heard from her for over eight months, but her last letter written in December on his birthday and received some two months later, told of how things were at the ranch and that all was well with them.

And there it was…..the Sabine River…...and Texas just on the other side.

Chapter Nineteen
The Running E in Sight

The Sabine River was easy to ford when Luke found a shallow point that would enable him to cross over without getting too wet. It was about three feet deep at that point, unusual for this time of the year, but a welcome exception anyway. Barely getting his boots damp, the first thing Luke did upon reaching the other side was to dismount and kneel in a short prayer of thanks for his safe deliverance after so many months of travel and for his life after so many battles. As he bowed his head, the locket that Elizabeth placed around his neck so many years ago swung forward to dangle just under his chin. He had not taken it off for four years and now it was reminding him once again that she would be waiting for him when he finally came home.

Patting the ground with his hand as a gesture to Texas that he was glad to be back on its soil, Luke stood up and remounted his horse with an elation that he had not felt for a very long time. He had felt a tremendous surge of energy when he left Appomattox and when he crossed the Mississippi River, but now, he had waded across the river which marked the Louisiana border and was finally back in his beloved Texas. Pulling the pocket watch from his pocket that his father had given him the day he left Texas, Luke noticed that it was nine thirty in the morning. "It's about time I returned home", he chuckled.

Remembering a time long ago when he first met Elizabeth and let out a long whoop on his return to the ranch, Luke stood up in the stirrups and at the top of his voice let loose with another "yeeeeehaaaaaa, I'm back in Texas again!"

The November sun was a welcome sight after so many days of rain that he had traveled through and warmed his body throughout. "With weather like this," he thought, I should be home before the end of the month."

The first town that Luke passed through was San Augustine just a few miles from the border he had just crossed. He knew that if he continued his westwardly direction that he would cross through the piney woods of east Texas before beginning the final stretch towards Austin over two hundred miles away. He still was counting on being home before the end of the month and predicted that he would definitely make it barring any unforeseen incident along the way.

The next several days passed quickly for Luke. He was making good time, his horse was still healthy, he was feeling wonderfully well, and the weather was holding.

As his mount climbed to the top of the next hill, Luke awoke from dozing in the saddle just in time to see Austin loom on the horizon. Taking his binoculars from his saddlebags, he strained to see the buildings he knew so well. "There's the capitol on top of the hill," he smiled and spoke to himself. "I'll need to cross the Colorado River on the ferry so that I can head on out to the ranch."

Remembering the first of the cold winds that blew across his face when he crossed the Mississippi River, Luke welcomed the breeze that now was on his face as he crossed the Colorado. It was a lot colder than the last one, but ever so welcome as the ferry inched it's way to the far side and the road to the ranch.

Passing through Salem in the late afternoon, Luke looked for familiar faces and recognized a few, but no one from the ranch to be seen. "They must all be at the ranch," he figured. Finally, the road to home was upon him and he knew that his family would be anxious to see him again.

The smoke from the chimney rose straight up in a curl and began to drift away with the slight northerly breeze that was sweeping the ranch. Elizabeth was in the kitchen with Lucy beginning to prepare dinner for that evening, William was on the sofa in the great room sipping a cup of coffee and reading the Austin paper from two days ago, Bill was playing with his toys as any four year old would do, and Micah was in the barn tending to the horses.

A strange sensation fell upon Elizabeth and she looked up from pealing the potatoes. Setting the knife gently down on the table she stared out the kitchen window for a few moments without moving. Just staring. Untying her apron, she let it drop to the floor in a heap, turned and walked towards the front door and hesitated. Placing her hand on the door latch for a few moments, she still was in wonderment as to the cause of this premonition she was having. She sensed something. She knew something was about to happen. Pulling the door open, Elizabeth stared out into the waning sunlight and observed nothing unusual there.

Closing the door behind her, she walked out into the yard and looked down the road leading towards Salem. Nothing. Nothing. Just the dusty road. Standing for a few moments with her hands in her pockets, she turned to walk back into the house when she took one last look down the road.

A lone figure riding tall in the saddle with a long rifle slung across the saddle came into view as Elizabeth looked long and hard at the approaching rider.

And there he was!

Screaming at the top of her voice, Elizabeth ran towards him calling "Luke! Luke! You're home! You're home!"

Dismounting and running to greet her, Luke grabbed her up and swung her around and around like they used to do as kids.

Neither said a word for a while. They just stood in the dusty road holding each other very close. Elizabeth began to cry a little, but Luke wiped the happy tears from her eyes as they both began to realize they were together again.

The November sun was just beginning to set out across the pasture and hills and the air was crisp and clean. A new day tomorrow and a new era was about to begin at the Running E once again.

Luke and Elizabeth walked towards the front door and Elizabeth looked up at Luke again. "My goodness, they are really going to be surprised when we walk in," she said with a twinkle.

The two of them opened the door together, took a couple of steps into the house, and just stopped. William looked up from reading his paper and could hardly believe his eyes. He just stared at them for a moment almost in disbelief until he realized that this was his son, home from the war, and safe once again. Dropping his newspaper, he raised his six foot two inch frame as if he had been pushed from his chair by some unknown hand and raced across the room to greet Luke standing there with Elizabeth. The two hugged each other for what seemed an hour when William, with a raspy voice and a tear in his eye said "my son, my son, welcome home."

Looking up from his toys that he had been playing with just moments before, Bill sprang up from his spot on the floor and ran to his own papa that he had never seen before, but knew from his mother's descriptions of him exactly who he was at first sight. Luke grabbed the handsome four year old in his arms, lifting him high above at arms length and exclaimed "you are a handsome young man, Bill. I can't tell you how glad I am to see you for the very first time. We've a lot of catching up to do and I aim to start right away." Clutching him ever so tightly, Luke could hardly believe that this was really his own son and he was seeing him for the very first time.

"He can already ride a horse all by himself," Elizabeth said proudly as she wiped a tear from her eye as well.

Hearing all the commotion, Lucy came out of the kitchen to see what was going on when she suddenly realized Luke stood before her holding Bill and smiling his big beautiful smile. Giving him a big welcome hug,

Lucy ran back to the kitchen saying she had to go find Micah to tell him the good news of his arrival.

Luke's first home cooked meal in over four years was a delicious feast for him and he could hardly believe that he was indeed back at the ranch and anxious to begin his interrupted life once again. He could hardly take his eyes off his new son and marveled throughout the homecoming dinner what a wonderful feeling it was to have him now as a new part of his family. Elizabeth sat most of the time in awe as she, too, could hardly believe her eyes that her Luke was sitting so near to her side once again. William sat watching also and thinking how lucky he was to have such a beautiful family. He also thought for a moment how much Susanna would have loved this moment of reunion that had been so long in the making.

Later that evening when all were seated around the fireplace savoring the moment, Luke took from the corner of the room a long canvas wrapped object that he had carried with him for so long. Unsheathing the Kentucky long rifle, Luke handed it to William proudly and said "it took very good care of me all these years, Papa, and I wanted to return it to you once again as I promised I would do." Digging into his pocket, he pulled the gold watch that his grandfather and father had both carried with them into battles and handed it to William and said "here's the other thing I promised I would return to you again when I came home. It, too, has been in a lot of battles, but it has come home like I have, safe and sound once again."

For Bill, Luke presented him with the binoculars he had carried with him and showed him how things far off in the pastures could appear almost within arms reach. Bill wore them around his neck for days and would not take them off saying he was just like his Papa.

Remembering the flowers he had pressed in his Bible when he left Vicksburg, he offered them to Elizabeth with the promise he would help her plant their seeds in the flower beds come next spring.

The next several days, Luke got used to home life again and welcomed the familiar routine he had longed for throughout the war. His backside was still sore and tired of riding so much having spent the last few months in the saddle as he made his way home to Texas. He just took long strolls with Elizabeth and Bill out in the pastures and down the dusty road. The days were much colder now that winter was upon them and nightly gatherings around the fireplace were where Luke began to recount the events of the war to Elizabeth and William. He told of the hardships, the battles, the terror, the destruction, the sniping from the trees, the fallen soldiers, and the awful food. He related his being promoted to Captain and of his meetings with General Lee and General Grant just prior to the surrender and of his long ride home from Virginia.

One evening, Luke went with Elizabeth to visit with Micah and Lucy and told them of the incident with Joshua. He felt as if he had to explain to them what had happened, but that he knew that Joshua had been taken care of by the Union soldiers. Luke asked if they had heard from him at all since he had left unexpectedly so long ago and their answer was that not one word had come from him. They were relieved at least that he was still all right towards the end of the war and hoped and prayed that he had made it to the end.

December was upon them and a new year not far behind. The war was over and a new beginning was in the offing.

Luke was home at last.

Chapter Twenty
A New Breed of Cattle

The Running E ranch welcomed the new year of 1870 with enthusiasm. The size of the ranch had continued to grow since Luke had returned from the war and was now approaching almost twenty thousand acres because of very wise investments in two smaller adjoining ranches that were sold to Luke. It was now one of the largest in the area and probably would grow even larger.

The Elliotts and the Wyatts were now in a partnership to raise Brahmans, a new breed of cattle not seen much before in central Texas, and were cross breeding them with herefords and angus in their search for a better grade of beef. The tough longhorn, the long established breed of the southwest, was beginning to fade from demand because of the new quality beef now called Brangus and Breford.

William had decided to retire from ranching three years ago and turned over the responsibilities of running the ranch totally to Luke and Elizabeth. He remained at the ranch for a year or so after his decision, but decided to move on in to Austin where he could be close to Sullivan who also was considering retiring from the legal profession. The two brothers were often seen at the local coffee shops on Congress Avenue discussing politics in general and Texas' future. He still missed Susanna very much and often would take a stroll along the river just to think of her.

Micah and Lucy were still helping to run the ranch. Micah was now totally gray headed and moved a little slower, but always reminded Luke that he could still outride him when roping cattle. After all, who taught him how in the first place! Luke never disagreed. They had not heard from Joshua for several years and didn't know if he was even still alive. But they still longed to see him again.

Luke and Elizabeth's family had grown to five. Elizabeth gave birth to twins, a boy and a girl, in late 1866 and named them Marshall Daniel and Susanna Lucy. The girl's names were selected because of the love they had not only for Luke's mother, but also for their lifelong friend, Joshua's mother.

The ranching business now was so successful that Luke had to make weekly trips to Austin to the bank and to Sullivan's office for legal papers. He usually drove his new surrey, but still preferred his horse and often would take it rather than travel in style. Less obvious, he always said since he still was not accustomed to the social status he and Elizabeth now enjoyed. They had become the talk of Austin and were often invited to events held at the Governor's Mansion or at one of the big hotels on Congress Avenue.

After signing several legal papers for the purchase of the other ranches, Luke left Sullivan's office and decided to stroll down Congress Avenue just because he felt like a good walk on this new spring day. So many of the townsfolk greeted him by name and Luke would always acknowledge them with a tip of his Stetson hat and a friendly return greeting. "Wish I could remember their names," Luke would say to himself after passing and promised himself he would try to do a better job of remembering those who held him in such awe.

Stopping for lunch down about where 6th Street crossed Congress, Luke turned into a small café and treated himself to a sandwich and some pecan pie for dessert. He remembered how he had missed pecan pie when he was gone and never passed up an opportunity to have a piece when it presented itself.

Finishing a second cup of coffee, Luke wiped his lips with his napkin and paid his bill for lunch as he headed out the door to continue his afternoon stroll. He decided to walk on down to the river and watch the boats go by for a while. He had always wanted to learn how to sail a boat and the sight of several on the river made him determined he would try it someday. "Time to head back to get my surrey" he mumbled, taking one last look at the small sailboats making a leisurely tack across the river.

Heading back up Congress Avenue, Luke stopped to watch the train come into the station. He had always loved to see it come in and stopped by often in the afternoons when in town just to watch all the people getting off.

The usual travelers stepped down from the train and Luke wondered where they had come from. Noticing a group of Union soldiers gathering on the platform, he admired their clean blue uniforms and their military bearing. He also remembered seeing that same uniform in his rifle's telescope, but put that memory fast out of his mind. The sergeant in charge was handing out discharge papers to the soldiers who were being released from military duty and wishing them well in civilian life. They all departed with a shout of glee and began to wander off the platform.

Turning to walk away from the station, Luke stopped dead in his tracks when something familiar about one of the soldiers became obvious. The soldier had his back to him, but Luke could tell that he was a Negro soldier who was then leaning over struggling to pick up his bag. Walking towards the soldier, Luke spoke in a soft voice "may I help you with that bag, soldier?"

"Why, thank you sir," the soldier replied and turned to face Luke.

They both stared at one another for a brief moment in disbelief. Then smiles broke out on both faces.

"Joshua!" Luke spoke with tears in his eyes.

"Luke!" replied Joshua also holding back his own tears.

They both gave each other a long hug interrupted by an occasional pat on the back before either one could speak.

The passersby on Congress Avenue hardly noticed the two men, one a soldier and the other a rancher, embracing one another as if they had found a long lost friend.

They had.

****

The ride back to the ranch was a joyous one. Luke and Joshua had talked almost incessantly from the time they first met at the station and Luke could hardly wait to reunite Joshua with his parents whom he hadn't seen for so long.

Joshua had been concerned that his parents wouldn't welcome him because of the way he had left the ranch back at the beginning of the war and run away to join the Union forces. Luke reassured him that his homecoming would be one of welcome and rejoicing for everyone.

Approaching the ranch, Luke prepared to turn into the drive leading up to the house when he saw Micah walking towards them a couple of hundred feet away. He, too, stopped in his tracks when he saw that there were two people in Luke's surrey and could hardly believe his own eyes when Joshua leapt from the surrey and ran to his father.

Spotting them from the kitchen window, Lucy ran from the house to greet Joshua followed by Elizabeth and the children. The happy reunion in the front yard was full of hugs, kisses, and tears of gratitude for Joshua's return home.

The next morning Luke was saddling up Golden to ride out to the north pasture when Joshua came into the stable. "Joshua, come along with me this morning I need to talk to you about something. Do you think you can still ride a horse?' Luke jokingly needled.

"Friend, I can still outride you on any day you choose, but I must admit I'm a little rusty at the moment," Joshua replied.

"I have a surprise for you" Luke grinned. Giving a sharp whistle, Apple came trotting into the stable and went straight to Joshua nuzzling him as he used to do so many years ago. They both were very glad to see one another again.

Saddling up, Joshua joined Luke as they headed out to check on the cattle in the pasture. They rode together just as they had done so many times in the past and both of them admitted how good it felt to be together once again.

"Joshua, your dad has mentioned that he would like to trim back on some of his foreman's duties because he felt that he was just getting a little too old to go out chasing after cattle much longer," Luke said. "Since I have added on so many new acres to the ranch and it seems to want to grow even more, I'm gonna need some real help runnin' this place. Elizabeth and I discussed this last night and she agrees that you are the only one who can take over the responsibilities to help me do this job and I would like to ask you to become my new ranch foreman when your dad hangs up his spurs. Would you even consider it?" Luke asked.

Joshua broke out in a big smile and told Luke it would be just like their fathers had done back in the beginnings of the Running E. "Luke, you are my best friend and always have been and to continue the management of this great ranch would be an honor for me to carry. But there is one thing I would like to do first," Joshua said.

"What's that?" Luke asked.

"Let's go fishing." Joshua answered.

"Just like old times, old friend", Luke added. "Just like old times."

The End!

About the Author

JOHN HAMLETT, a retired Navy officer and presently a substitute elementary school teacher, began his writing career in Houston at age 14 with his own weekly column as a teenage reporter for two large Houston newspapers. He is the author of "Pigtails and Inkwells", a collection of stories he tells his schoolchildren of how life was during the 1940s when he was their age.

He lives in the Dallas suburb of Richardson with his wife, Elly. Their children and grandchildren live there also.